They drew to a halt outside a grey stone farmhouse.

'You two come in and have a cup of something hot, and we will get a room ready for you,' the farmer ordered.

They were bustled inside and provided with mugs of steaming cocoa while Nick relayed their sorry tale. By the time he'd finished the farmer's wife had returned and was beckoning them.

'We don't want to put you out,' Nick began.

'No problem. The bed has already been made up.'

'Bed?' Adele squeaked, and Nick elbowed her firmly in the ribs. They were safe and warm, and she'd been perfectly happy to snuggle up half an hour ago. They'd just have to share.

They were led outside and across a yard to a square stone building with a heavy-beamed door. Inside was surprisingly cosy. There was a small sitting room and kitchen on the lower level, and up a curling flight of stairs was a bedroom with *en-suite* bathroom. Fluffy towels sat on the end of the bed, and the duvet looked about a foot deep. Nick felt relaxed just looking at it. And before he knew it he and Adele were standing alone in the room, either side of the huge brass bed, staring at each other...

Dear Reader

I wanted to write a story that started after the traditional fairytale ending—one that began *after* the wedding vows. Keeping hold of that 'happy ever after' can be tricky, even if the couple in question is clearly meant to be together—as Adele and Nick are in BREAK UP TO MAKE UP.

Nick was great fun to write. He's a fun-loving, risk-taking charmer, and has a cheeky sense of humour that often gets him into trouble—especially with his soon-to-be ex-wife Adele, a buttoned-up businesswoman who is struggling to maintain her perfect image. I'm sure, as twenty-first century women, we can all relate to the pressure to prove we can 'have it all'.

I got the initial idea for the setting for this book after watching a documentary on British television about how a whole motorway was brought to a standstill one night by a light dusting of snow. What a great place for a warring couple to be stranded, I thought to myself. There'll be no getting away from the issues they're trying to avoid if they're stuck in a car together. Although the storyline changed as I wrote the book, there's still a reference to the original news story that sparked the idea in the first place. See if you can spot it!

Fiona Harper

BREAK UP TO MAKE UP

BY
FIONA HARPER

MILLS & BOON®

First published in Great Britain 2007
Harlequin Mills & Boon Limited,
Eton House, 18-24 Paradise Road, Richmond, Surrey TW9 1SR

© Fiona Harper 2007

ISBN-13: 978 0 263 19647 4

Set in Times Ror
07-0607-54022

Printed and bound in Great Britain
by Antony Rowe Ltd, Chippenham, Wiltshire

As a child, **Fiona Harper** was constantly teased for either having her nose in a book, or living in a dream world. Things haven't changed much since then, but at least in writing she's found a use for her runaway imagination. After studying dance at university, Fiona worked as a dancer, teacher and choreographer, before trading that career in for video-editing and production. When she became a mother she cut back on her working hours to spend time with her children, and when her littlest one started pre-school she found a few spare moments to rediscover an old but not forgotten love—writing.

Fiona lives in London, but her other favourite places to be are the Highlands of Scotland and the Kent countryside on a summer's afternoon. She loves cooking, good food and anything cinnamon-flavoured. Of course she still can't keep away from a good book, or a good movie—especially romances—but only if she's stocked up with tissues, because she knows she will need them by the end, be it happy or sad. Her favourite things in the world are her wonderful husband, who has learned to decipher her incoherent ramblings, and her two daughters.

Fiona has a love/hate relationship with her husband's satellite navigation system, and it provided her with ammunition—sorry, inspiration—for this story. Everything the infernal machine does in BREAK UP TO MAKE UP is based on a real-life occurrence.

For Janine, my ever-capable friend,
who gave me inspiration

CHAPTER ONE

ADELE fought the urge to run from the bathroom screaming. She closed her eyes, took a deep breath and ordered her hands to stop shaking. When she felt her heart rate slow a little, she opened her eyes again.

Nothing had changed. Eight legs and a fat, hairy body still inhabited her bath. She took a few steps backwards, never letting her gaze off the spindly legs, checking for any twitch that indicated it was thinking of making a sudden move.

Once the edge of the tub obscured her view of the intruder, she fumbled on the shelf above the sink. Toothpaste and toothbrush went flying as she grabbed the glass they sat in. All she needed now was something flat and not too flexible. Her eyes darted round the room, hardly taking anything in. She made herself look again, more slowly this time.

Balanced on the washing hamper was the magazine she'd been reading last time she'd been having one of her ritual soaks. The sort of soak she ought to be having right now, if it weren't for the intruder. Righteous anger bubbled in her chest. How dare that nasty little…squatter…spoil her plans for the evening?

She seized the magazine and marched towards the bath, trying not to let her steps falter as she drew close. It had been much easier when she'd had someone else to do her spider-

catching. But those days were gone. This was between her and
eight-legged Freddy over there.

She lifted the upturned glass in her hand, hoping it wasn't
going to slip. Even her fingertips seemed sweaty. Her breath
came in gasps, punctuated by long gaps when the air stayed
locked in her chest. Two more steps and she'd be close
enough.

The glass was only inches away from the creature now.
Everything went very still. Even the spider—as if it sensed
her approach. And then it darted. Straight towards her up the
side of the bath.

Adele didn't stop to think; she just threw both glass and
magazine in the direction of her attacker and raced out of the
bathroom. And while the sound of shattering glass echoed in
her ears, she slammed the door and leant against it. Just in
case it was thinking of trying the door handle.

See? This was why she shouldn't be doing this! Her phobia
made her irrational. She would have moved away from the
door at that point, but a noise from inside the bathroom made
her grip the door handle tighter.

If only...

No, she wasn't going to do it. She wasn't going to wish
him here.

She did not need a man to catch a spider. Especially *that* man.

Her fingers forgot the door knob as she let out a long sigh
and ran them through her long dark hair.

I can do this, she thought as she stood there in the silence.
I've got to. No one else is going to do it for me.

Her hands shook as she smoothed down the folds of her
spotlessly white towelling bathrobe and tightened the sash.
It was a pointless gesture. Her furry friend in there didn't care
what she looked like, but somehow she needed to present a
calm and cool front, to be the Adele she knew how to be, the
Adele who wasn't fazed by anything or anyone.

She turned to face the bathroom door and imagined herself in one of her business suits, her hair in its usual coil at the nape of her neck, not fanning over her shoulders and falling over her face. It was all about mental attitude, wasn't it? You could do anything if you put your mind to it.

She'd been sent on some stupid training seminar when she'd worked at Fenton and Barrett. She had pretended she was listening, but really she'd been plotting how she was going to start her own firm of management consultants. She'd made her dreams come true since then and she could certainly use the same trick now.

What had those people waffled on about? Oh, yes. Visualisation. She concentrated, and in her mind's eye the creature in the bath became a butterfly, brightly coloured and fragile.

Anyone could pick up a butterfly, couldn't they?

She wrenched the door open and marched over to the bath. Shattered glass covered the bottom, but the creature she sought was now halfway up the side under the taps. If she didn't know better she'd think it was giving her a cocky look.

'Butterfly,' she murmured under her breath as she extended her hand forward and closed her fingers over it. The distance from the edge of the bath to the window suddenly stretched to the size of a football pitch. She tried to walk slowly, but after a step and a half she was running. 'Butterfly!' she shouted as the legs started to twitch in her hand and she fought the reflex to gag.

'Yuck! Spider, spider, spider, spider!' she yelled as she opened the catch with her free hand and threw the horrible thing out of the window. Then she shivered and rubbed her hand on her robe over and over again until she thought she'd wear the little loops away.

She *really* needed that bath now. But before she could do that, there was a whole lot of glass to clean up. There was no

one here to catch spiders and there was no one here to pull
the shards out of her bottom if she missed a bit, so she'd better
do a good job.

Her head was practically in the cupboard under the kitchen
sink when the doorbell rang. The sun had only just set and it
was light enough not to have to turn the lamps on, but dark
enough not to be able to see what she was looking for. Her
fingers stretched into the shadows at the back of the cupboard.

Where was that darn dustpan and brush? It had to be here
somewhere.

The bell went again and Adele banged her head on the top
of the cupboard. She did not have the kind of doorbell you
could ignore, all soft chimes, indicating someone was waiting
patiently at the door, flowers in hand. Oh, no. This was one
of those insistent ones that grated like an old-fashioned
bicycle bell.

All she'd wanted to on a Saturday evening, after spending
all day at the office, was to sink into a silky rich bubble bath
and read the next four chapters of her book. That wasn't too
much to ask, was it?

She rubbed the back of her head as she took silent, quick
steps to the front door and yanked it open, not even caring
she was in her bathrobe.

She was going to deliver a brisk 'Yes? What do you want?'
But the words died on her lips. Leaning against the wall, with
a twinkle in his eyes and a dimple in each cheek, was the most
infuriating man she'd ever had the displeasure of knowing.

She knew her mouth was hanging open, but she couldn't
seem to get it closed again. He smiled and the dimples
deepened.

'Hi, Adele.'

'N…Nick!'

In the last few minutes the sun had tucked itself even
further below the suburban skyline of slate roofs and chimney

pots and the glow from the porch light made him seem warm and golden in contrast.

He looked so…real. Not like the Nick she'd been scream- ing at in her head for the past nine months, anyway. In her memory she'd made him shorter, more boyish and much less attractive. She could feel the familiar chemistry starting to frazzle her brain already.

He looked deep into her eyes and she felt another few brain cells pop into nothingness.

He hitched an eyebrow. 'The one and only.'

She shook her head, not even knowing where to start. Why was he here? How long had he been back in the country? And more importantly, why was he standing on her front doorstep as if nothing had ever happened?

'Can I come in?'

She wanted to slam the door in his face, tell him he could get lost and contact her through her solicitor if he had to, but somehow she found herself nodding. He'd always seemed to have the irritating knack of getting her to go along with almost anything he said. And although he meant well, she was the one who always seemed to end up getting hurt or having to tidy up the resulting mess.

It had been a really bad idea to let Nick Hughes into her life.

It had been an even worse idea to marry him.

Adele marched down the hall and Nick followed. She turned to face him once they got into the kitchen. 'What do you want, Nick?'

This was the moment he'd been waiting for, the moment he'd rehearsed so many times in his head he'd lost count. Never once in all his daydreams had he felt this nervous.

Adele turned to look at him and he tried not to wince. He'd been afraid of this. He'd hoped that after all this time she'd be in more of a mood to talk. Obviously not. Time had made no impact whatsoever on the healing process.

Diving right in and telling her why he was here wasn't going to work; he would have to build up to it slowly. He swallowed the heartfelt plea on his lips and replaced it with the widest, cheekiest smile he could muster.

'That's a nice way to greet your husband.'

Adele's eyes narrowed.

He took a deep breath. He had to do something to stop her throwing him out on his ear. Somehow he had to stay in the same building as her long enough to get her to listen. The urge to wise-crack was overpowering, like an itch begging to be scratched, but he managed to mumble something less inflammatory.

'How about a cup of tea?'

She just continued to stare at him, her pupils shrinking to pinpricks. OK, not one of his best efforts, but his brain was like fudge after what seemed like a week on a plane and a cup of tea would give him at least another fifteen minutes to talk Adele round.

'I've had a really long trip,' he added.

She stayed as still and hard and cold as the granite on the kitchen worktops. And just when he thought she'd solidified and was going to stay like that for ever, she shook her head and marched over to the kettle. He kept a very close eye on her. When Adele was in this kind of mood, she was just as likely to throw the kettle at him as she was to switch it on.

She filled it with water, her back still to him, as she repeated her earlier question.

'What do you want, Nick?'

He waited until she turned to face him.

'We need to talk.'

Nothing funny about that statement. It seemed his valiant efforts to ignore the old joke-when-stressed reflex were paying off.

She shook her head. 'No. We needed to talk months ago. It's too late.'

'I've got something important I need to discuss with you.'

'Hah!'

He flinched. 'What do you mean, *hah*?'

'You don't *do* important, though, do you, Nick? Or responsible, or reliable, or anything that might involve getting serious in the slightest.'

Adele was on the attack. All his good intentions crumbled and he resorted to the only form of defence that worked. A slow smile turned the corners of his mouth up. 'It's part of my charm.'

'It's why our marriage fell apart.'

There wasn't a flicker of a smile on her lips. It definitely wasn't going the way he'd planned. He was so tired he could hardly think straight and he tried the one thing left in his arsenal that was guaranteed to get a reaction.

Desperate times called for desperate measures. It was time to break out the dimples.

He widened his smile just that little bit more and watched Adele's eyes closely to see if he could detect a thaw. She couldn't resist his dimples.

'Stop it, Nick.'

The air of innocence in his shrug should have won him an Oscar.

'I know what you're doing and it's not going to work.'

That'd be a first. Obviously Adele had grown another inch of armour plating while he'd been away. But there were always chinks; it was just a case of locating them. It was one of the things that had attracted him to her in the first place, the frosty outer shell hiding a scorching core. Fire and ice—that was Adele.

He walked towards her and she backed away from him. 'You said you wanted to talk? Well, I'm busy at the moment.'

'I can see.' He looked her up and down and felt a familiar surge of heat as he saw one shapely leg revealed by the split in her bathrobe.

Adele straightened and yanked the knot of the sash even tighter. 'Call me at the office next week. I'm in the middle of a big project, but I may have a few minutes to spare on Thursday. Where are you going to be staying?'

Nick raised his eyebrows and looked around the room.

'No way! You are not staying here.'

He blinked. 'It's my home too.'

'Correction. It might be your *house*, but it stopped being your *home* the moment you waltzed off across the Atlantic and didn't bother to come back for nine months.'

Adele crossed her arms and looked at him. Now was not the time to remind her that he *had* come back, as soon as he'd been able to. Two short weeks after their massive fight, he'd travelled five thousand miles to patch things up. But he'd walked into the house and found it empty. Adele had moved out and was staying with her best friend.

No, it wouldn't do to remind her. She wasn't in the mood to be confronted with her mistakes at the moment. To be honest, he didn't think he could face the memories either. So he tucked them away at the back of his brain and ignored the sick feeling building in the pit of his stomach.

He took off his jacket, slung it over the back of one of the chairs surrounding the big pine dining table and dropped into the squashy sofa tucked into the corner of their country-style kitchen.

He was in a big enough hole as it was. He might just as well carry on digging. Anything to keep her mind off shoving his six-foot frame through the front door. Adele might be petite, but she was surprisingly strong.

'How about that tea?'

Adele closed her eyes and her shoulders sagged. He'd won

the first round, but he felt like kicking himself in the behind for making her look so tired and world-weary.

'Get it yourself. I'm going upstairs. And if you think you're putting that bag you dumped in the hallway in *my* bedroom you can think again. You know where the spare room is.'

Ouch.

Nick grimaced as Adele spun round and stomped up the stairs. He had not handled that well, but arguing back would have made her dig her heels in deeper. He'd learned long ago that getting her to laugh was the solution.

She had a good sense of humour; she just kept it on a tight leash most of the time. And if there was one thing he was good at, it was making his wife smile.

Seeing Adele defrost was a wonderful thing. She started off all spiky and hard—like one of those puffer fish—and he'd just keep being impossible until he could see the glint in her eyes and the way her jaw worked overtime to keep a straight face. If he timed it right, he'd give one last smile, one last look, and she'd let out a big puff of air and deflate, becoming the warm, passionate woman he loved so much.

He let his head fall back onto the sofa cushion and closed his eyes.

He knew what she thought: that her husband had chosen a once-in-a-lifetime job over her, but that wasn't the way he saw it at all. Adele was too busy being self-righteous to see that *she* was the one who had refused to budge an inch. It had been her decision to put the marriage on hold.

There might be two sides to every story, but Adele was always, always convinced hers was the right one. The annoying thing was, most of the time she *was* right. However, now and again she got things spectacularly wrong. And when she did, it was usually something big.

He wiggled into a more comfortable position. The jet lag was catching up on him and this sofa was so comfy. The jacket of one of her business suits was draped across the back. It smelled of her perfume, warm and spicy. If he closed his eyes, it was almost as if she were sitting next to him.

They'd spent many happy evenings cuddled up together on this old sofa with glasses of wine after the evening meal was finished. And there had been other times when they used the sofa for much less relaxing pursuits...

He smiled to himself as he drifted off to sleep. Less relaxing, but so much more fun.

The kitchen door creaked slightly as Adele pushed it open. She paused. It was quiet. Too quiet. Nick was like a naughty toddler in that respect. If he was silent, he was probably up to no good. The door swung wide and she spotted him, sprawled all over the sofa, sleeping like a baby.

Even that made her want to scream. How did he do that? Turn off all the tension between them and lapse into unconsciousness? She was nowhere near relaxed. Drink ten espressos—doubles— and you'd have an idea of where her nerve levels were. Then she looked at Nick again and a sigh left her chest unbidden.

Fast asleep like that, he looked so angelic. His hair was just that little bit too long to be spiky and there always seemed to be a bit that fell across his forehead. Many a time she'd woken early in the morning, smiled at him and brushed the wayward strand away. It was all she could do at that very moment to stop herself crossing the room and repeating the gesture.

She had to get out of here. Now. Before she forgot all the reasons why Nick Hughes should not be let within a five-mile radius of her heart.

She grabbed her handbag off the counter and closed the kitchen door. Moments later she was fully kitted out in coat, scarf and gloves and was making her way down the road. Mid-February in London was invariably damp and cold, and this night was happy to follow the trend.

She found herself at Mona's house. Her precariously balanced life had just fallen off a precipice and she needed her best friend. Mona answered the door with a baby on her hip.

'My God, Adele! What's happened?'

'It's Nick.'

Mona gasped and put a hand to her mouth. 'Is he…? Was there an accident?'

'No. Worse.'

'Worse than falling off the side of a mountain?'

'I've no idea whether he's been climbing or not recently, but I do know where he is right this very minute. My extreme-sports-loving husband is alive and well and fast asleep in our kitchen—my kitchen.'

Mona's brows gathered together like thunderclouds. She pulled Adele into a gruff hug that was both sudden and un-expected. 'You'd better come in and tell me all about it.'

When Adele pulled away she had baby drool on the front of her jacket. She stroked her goddaughter's head and gave her a kiss then let Mona lead her into the sitting room.

'He just turned up out of the blue.'

'No warning at all?'

Adele gave her friend a knowing look. 'What? Nick? The man who is so bad at forward planning that he can't even decide what he wants to eat for dinner until he's hungry?'

Mona popped Bethany on the floor and gave her a rattle to play with. 'What does he want?'

Adele shrugged. 'Who knows? I tried asking him, but he just got all…Nick…on me. He says he wants to talk.'

'About what?'

Adele let out a breath and felt her stomach plunge down-wards. 'I suppose he could be back to ask for a…you know…divorce,' she said quietly. 'That would explain why he didn't just want to launch into it. Even Nick wouldn't just turn up after nine months—'

'Nine and a half, actually.'

Adele closed her eyes briefly and shook her head. 'Well, however many months... Even Nick wouldn't just turn up and say, *Hi, honey, I'm home—and, by the way, you're history.*'

Mona nodded. 'Of course, you'll want to get in first.'

Her friend looked so serious Adele dared not mention that she hadn't thought of that. But she should have. Where was her old fighting spirit? Suddenly the furnace of indignation was about as lively as the rain-soaked coals on a typical English barbecue.

Mona sat back and gave her a questioning look.

'Please don't tell me you want him back!'

A reflex answer should have popped out of Adele's mouth at that second. A firm *no*. Of course not. Never in a million years. Instead she closed her eyes and rubbed the sides of her face with her hands.

'Adele?'

'I thought I wanted him gone for good. It was an easy decision when he was thousands of miles away, but now he's back and...I don't know...divorce just seems so...final.'

'Don't you dare let him wear you down with that boyish charm of his, Adele!'

'I'm not!'

'Pah! You're weakening. I can see the cracks from here. Have you forgotten how he treated you when he left?'

No, she hadn't forgotten. She remembered every last detail of the day he'd dropped the bombshell.

His work as a special-effects designer for TV and films had really been taking off, after years of only just scraping by. Seemed he'd actually been doing more than just messing around in the shed at the bottom of the garden with bits of scrap metal and rubbery stuff.

After a couple of popular TV commercials, he'd been asked to do the effects for a low-budget independent film.

Against all expectation, the film had been a huge hit and Nick's name had been put firmly on the map. They'd both been so pleased at the time. She'd even been able to put up with the strange hours and the fact he could disappear for days at a time, often arriving back with no warning at four in the morning. If she'd have known what was going to come of all of it, she might not have been so thrilled for him.

One day, he'd burst into her office and announced the big news, wearing a grin so wide she'd thought his face would split. He'd been offered a job on a big Hollywood project, some sci-fi film, and he had five days to pack and get himself out to California to meet with the producers. If they liked him, he needed to start almost straight away.

That was when things started to go seriously wrong. Nick had been so busy in the following months that Adele had almost felt as if she were single again. Often the only evidence that he'd come home at all when she woke up in the mornings were the plans for the next contraption he was going to build doodled in the margins of one of her reports.

And then he'd wanted her to leave her business behind and move halfway across the world at a moment's notice. As if. For the first time in her life she'd had roots. A home. A purpose. There was no way she was going to throw all of that away on a whim. It had been time to put her foot down.

They'd had a huge fight. The worst one they'd ever had—and that was saying something. Even so, when she'd yelled, 'Take the stupid job if you really think it's that important!' she hadn't expected him to take her at her word and jump on a plane.

Mona's voice brought her back to the present. 'Come on, girl. You've got to be strong.'

'I am strong,' Adele said, her face drooping. At least, she wanted to be. Month upon month of pretending she'd been fine without Nick had been exhausting.

Mona's husband had upped and left when baby number two had arrived only ten months ago. She and Mona had got through the early months of their individual crises by channelling their anger into weekly ranting sessions in Mona's front room.

The period after Nick had left had been the worst in her life and she was not going to give him the opportunity to send her spiralling back to that dark, lonely place.

She sat up straighter. 'No, you're right. Who needs men? Stuff 'em!'

'That's more like it. Now, how are you going to deal with the daredevil who's currently snoozing in your kitchen?'

Fire him into next week with one of his homemade canons?

Tempting. Very tempting, in fact. She should encourage that feeling, let it grow and swell, and then she wouldn't do the other thing she was sorely temped to do—run back home just to look at him while he slept. Kiss him awake and show him how much she'd missed him.

But she couldn't weaken like that. She wouldn't.

He'd done the one thing he'd promised never to do: he'd left her, and she wasn't about to give him the chance to hurt her that way again. At least, that was what her head was telling her. Her heart had a crazy agenda all of its own.

Adele shook her head. 'I suppose I'm going to have to go and talk to him at some point. I just can't face it tonight. When Nick catches me on the hop, I always end up agreeing to one of his crazy schemes. I need to be prepared. Focused.'

She could not let Nick know he still had the power to make her quiver every time he came near. He'd use it against her. He'd make her believe they'd have a chance then he'd yank the rug right from under her feet again. It was inevitable.

She needed to protect herself. Nick had to believe she was totally immune to him and there was no way she was going to convince him of that tonight. She was still in a state of shock and likely to do something stupid—like tell him she'd been joking about the spare room.

'Stay here,' Mona said. 'We can make battle plans over a bottle of red wine.'

'Thanks, Mona. You're a lifesaver.'

Mona picked up Bethany, who was starting to grizzle, and stood up. 'Come on, young miss. Time for bed.' She turned just before she headed out of the living-room door.

'Does he know about…you know?'

Adele threaded her fingers together and squeezed until her knuckles hurt. 'No. I never told him.'

CHAPTER TWO

THERE WAS A HAND brushing his face. Nick sat up, suddenly wide awake, and realised the fingers were his own. He had hooked his elbow behind his head while he'd been sleeping and now his hand felt fat and numb.

The lights were still on in the kitchen, but it was dark outside and he had no idea what time it was. He shook his dead hand until he could feel the blood prickle then took a look at his watch. Six a.m. No way!

He shook his head and looked again. No wonder he felt so stiff. He'd spent the last twelve hours on a two-seater sofa, crunched into goodness-knew-what strange positions.

Adele would probably be up in an hour or so. She had always been an early riser, a complete contrast to his night-owlish tendencies. He felt crumpled and stale, not just from his strange sleeping place, but also from the long flight from LA the day before. No point trying to sweet talk Adele if he was looking rough and smelling even worse. He'd better hop in the shower and spruce up before he tried talking to her again.

He dragged his bag upstairs, and almost barged into the master bedroom on autopilot. An idiotic mistake. He'd have to think quicker than that if he wanted to get on Adele's good side. Even he wasn't daft enough to think he could jump back into his life after all this time as if nothing had changed.

Only he wished he *could* just slide back into his old life. He and Adele had been so happy. One moment of rash anger had probably cost him his marriage. He hardly ever lost his temper, but Adele had pushed and pushed and pushed until he'd erupted.

It just proved to him that his usual technique of sweeping everything negative under the carpet and wisecracking until it all went away was a much safer option. If he'd done that last May, maybe things would have been different. He wouldn't have had to live with the ache deep inside that just wouldn't go away, no matter how many practical jokes he'd played on his colleagues to distract himself from it.

Half an hour later he was shaved, dressed and making coffee in the kitchen. The idea was to catch Adele on the caffeine high after her obligatory morning coffee. He knew all the little tricks to get her onside, had employed them so many times it was almost habit.

Of course, this time he had to be extra careful. It was a bit more serious than the incident in which he'd finished off her designer make-up in an attempt to get a latex head he was about to split with an axe to look a little more lifelike.

And then, of course, there had been the time he'd used her best casserole to mix up gungy alien blood. She had not appreciated the green food colouring that wouldn't come off no matter how hard she'd scrubbed. He'd learned the hard way to stay clear of Adele's kitchen utensils. She was unusually finicky in that area.

No, this time he was going to be sensible and talk properly to her. That was plan A. Then he had to get her to agree to plan B, which hopefully would lead to fulfilling plan C. Plan C was the big one: making Adele see they were meant to be together.

He just couldn't fail at that one, so he was going to pull out all the stops. It couldn't hurt to smooth the way a little—with caffeine and smiles and dimples.

He turned the coffee machine on and sat himself at the table, opposite the door. Any moment now, she'd appear.

But Adele didn't appear. And patience was not one of Nick's strong suits.

Perhaps his wife would like breakfast in bed? Or was that taking the schmoozing a bit too far? When he'd left, Adele had not been one for Sunday-morning lie-ins. Not unless he'd been there to convince her there was something worth staying in bed for.

He leant back in the wooden chair, deflated. He'd missed Adele. Really missed her. When he'd got back to California after his first trip home, he'd been surprised how long the anger had bubbled inside him. He hadn't been able to shake it off as normal. But then, that was understandable, wasn't it?

Anyone would be angry if their wife had dumped them at the first tiny hiccup. They could have worked something out about their jobs and his six-month contract in Hollywood, but she hadn't even bothered to consider it. She'd been too busy screeching at him about how important her job and her life and her friends were to her. It had come as a rude shock to find that he was bottom of the list—if he was on there at all.

His job was just as important to him, but Adele never took him seriously, even when someone had pulled out of a contract and he'd been offered a last-minute chance to work with highly acclaimed producer Tim Brookman. He was practically Hollywood royalty. It had been an opportunity he just couldn't refuse, and it hurt more than he cared to admit that she hadn't enough faith in him to support his decision.

Irritation started to buzz round his head. He swatted it away and checked the clock. It was half-past eight now. Surely Adele wasn't still sleeping? Perhaps he'd better go and check she was OK.

He raced up the stairs, but slowed his pace as he neared their bedroom door. He smiled as he remembered the way she snored softly sometimes. It was so sweet. And it was strangely gratifying to know that perfect Adele had one tiny flaw.

But there was no snoring now. In fact, there was no sound at all.

He nudged the door open and blinked as he saw the room was unusually bright. The curtains were drawn and cold February sunshine lit up the empty bed. The covers were neatly in place and the elaborate arrangement of scatter cushions at the head of the bed was undisturbed.

His stomach bottomed out, just the way it had when he'd walked into the bedroom almost a year ago and seen the empty wardrobe, doors flung wide, hangers bare like autumn twigs.

Then he'd found the crisp, polite note saying she was staying at Mona's and didn't want to see him. He'd turned around and gone back to America, appalled his wife had bailed out on him so easily. At least he'd managed to persuade Mona to get her to move back into the house after he'd left.

He marched over to the wardrobe and wrenched the door open. Breath whooshed out of his lungs as he found the neat row of jackets, blouses and dresses—grouped by function and then by colour. If Adele found a pair of cargo trousers among her summer dresses, she'd get all itchy about it.

Now he was just plain confused. Adele's clothes were here, but Adele wasn't.

He turned and headed back downstairs and was just at the bottom step when he heard the front door open.

Adele jumped back, startled.

What the heck was going on?

Adele's face turned a fiery red and she was unusually flustered.

A horrible thought scratched at the back of his mind to be let in.

'Have you been out all night, Adele?'

She fumbled with the Sunday paper tucked under her arm. 'I think that falls into the category of *none of your business, don't you?'*

None of his…? The woman was priceless!

'You're still my wife!'

She refolded the newspaper and gave him a long, hard look. 'Well, we can always do something about that.'

Nick saw an uncharacteristic flash of red behind his eyes. Seismic activity he was surprised she could still provoke after all this time. He stormed through the house, down the garden path and into his workshop, slamming the door behind him.

None of his business!

He should have stayed to have it out with her, but his feet had been moving before his brain had engaged. He didn't feel much like going back into the house now, anyway.

Ethel, the shop mannequin he'd rescued from a skip, was still holding a pose in the corner of his workshop. At least she was predictable. Once upon a time, he'd have sworn Adele was too, but her refusal to compromise about his job had shattered that illusion. Like the dummy, he'd discovered she could be hard and cold in a way that had taken him totally by surprise.

'What do you think my chances are, Ethel? I need a woman's perspective.'

Ethel stared out of the window, her bright blue eyelids unblinking.

Nick sighed and fiddled with the soldering iron sitting on the bench.

'Yeah. Thanks for nothing, babe.'

Adele was working on her laptop when Nick came to find her. She was still all jittery after their confrontation in the hall. She'd almost faltered—almost. But in the end she'd managed to pull herself together and Nick would never know how close she'd come to soothing his anger away with a kiss.

She tried to pretend she wasn't aware of him standing in the doorway of the little box room they used as a study.

'I'm busy, Nick,' she said eventually, without looking round.

'We've got to talk some time.'

She shrugged and tried to concentrate on the words on the screen. None of them seemed to be recognisable as English any more. She read a sentence for the third time then gave up.

'OK. We'll talk.' She swivelled round in her chair and folded her arms. 'Fire away.'

Nick shook his head. 'Not like this. Let's get onto neutral territory. How about I take you out to lunch?'

Once upon a time, she'd loved spending long, lazy Sunday lunches with Nick. They'd sit outside in the pub garden in summer and huddle up to the fire inside in winter. She didn't want to be reminded of happier days, but he was right. They had to talk at some point and she might as well get it out of the way.

'OK, but you're paying.'

'Of course.'

Nick flashed his dimples and Adele had the feeling she was agreeing to a whole heap of trouble.

'What's this all about, then, Nick?'

They'd sat through most of the main course talking about nothing. Whether that was a good thing or not, she wasn't sure. All she knew was that the small talk was getting to her and she had to know one way or the other. Her heart broke into a trot at the thought of the 'D' word that might come out of his mouth. Bizarrely, it was the last word she wanted to hear, despite the fact it had been the one at the forefront of her mind since last summer.

Nick played with a roast potato on his plate.

'It's Mum's sixty-fifth birthday this year.'

Adele nodded. 'I know.' Then she frowned.

What was he up to? She leaned forward and tried to catch his gaze. He seemed to be absorbed in shepherding all his peas into a little pile with his knife.

'How is Maggie?'

She'd been a bit of a coward on that front after Nick had left. Everyone knew she was useless at keeping up with correspondence and she'd hidden behind that as an excuse to keep contact with Nick's family to a minimum. Yes, she'd dashed off the odd email and sent a Christmas card, but she'd avoided the messages on the answering machine, pretending to herself she was too busy with her work. In the last few months, everything had gone a little quiet.

The truth was, she was just plain scared. Scared, now she and Nick were no longer a couple, that maybe his mother and sisters would go cold on her. Just as her own parents had. She'd only been part of the family by default, after all. It had been easier to avoid anything deep than risk finding out her fears had some foundation.

He poked the pile of peas with his knife and sent them scattering. 'You know Mum…'

Adele tried not to let the shame show on her face. She'd been a coward, plain and simple.

She knew Nick's mother better than she knew her own. Which wasn't difficult, seeing as the last time she'd seen her parents in the flesh was a good three years ago. But that was nothing unusual. It had been that way since they'd packed her off to boarding-school so her mother could flit around the world with her father as he moved from exotic location to exotic location with his job.

Maggie Hughes was the sort of woman she'd fantasised about having as a parent in her teenage years. Her house was always full of children and grandchildren, who complained constantly that she had her nose in their business just a little too much, but it never seemed to stop them coming. She had a big heart and had made sure Adele always felt part of the family, always felt wanted. She was a little too indulgent with her only son, perhaps, but nobody was perfect.

'Give her my love when you speak to her, won't you?'

Nick coughed. 'Well, I was kind of thinking you could tell her yourself—in person.'

'And when would that be, exactly? You haven't forgotten with all your Hollywood high-flying that she moved in with Auntie Beverley last year, have you? Scotland is a long way to go for a cup of tea and a chat.'

'She's having a big birthday bash. Charlotte is organising it and, of course, my other sisters have been roped in too.'

Adele could imagine it. Nick had three older sisters. They were a formidable force *en masse*. Their only weakness was a huge soft spot for their baby brother. She'd heard plenty of stories about the scrapes Nick had got himself into as a cheeky young lad, and for every misdemeanour there was a matching tale of how one or all of the sisters had bailed him out, duffed up the bully, or cleaned up the resulting mess.

'What's this party got to do with me?'

Nick looked at her from under the wayward tuft of hair. 'Mum wants you to come. In fact, she's insisting.'

'Why?' Maggie was always so sensible. 'Surely she knows that having both of us together at the party would just make things awkward. Why would she want to risk her big night like that?'

'Er—that's the thing, you see. I haven't really told her about…us.'

Adele felt the band of tension across her forehead tighten a few notches. 'Us?'

'About our…you know…problems.'

The plate on the table swam before her eyes. The sinking feeling that he'd done it again—walked away from a difficult

situation, leaving someone else to deal with the fallout—
crept up on her and sat on her shoulder whispering nasty
little words in her ear.

Surely, not even Nick could be that daft? She looked at
him. That lopsided cocky smile said it all. He always pulled
that one out of the bag when he knew he'd done something
that was going to make her blood boil.

It was all Adele could do not to pick up his plate and pour
the contents, gravy and all, over his head. She should have
had a medal for managing to stand up and walk stiffly from
the restaurant without spontaneously combusting.

She gulped in a lungful of winter air and hoped it would
cool her down before he caught her up. She did not want to
make a huge scene in the car park of The Partridge.

This was typical Nick! Why had she even let him open his
mouth in the first place? She had known no good could come
of it, yet she'd trotted down the road with him like the class-
A doormat that she was.

She caught a flash of a brown leather jacket at the corner
of her eye and knew Nick had managed to pay the bill and
give chase.

Well, tough. She wasn't ready to talk to him right now.
Thankfully, they'd decided to walk down the road to the
nearest pub for lunch. It would only take her ten minutes to
get home.

She listened to the staccato rhythm of her boots on the
pavement as she stalked off in the direction of the house.
Make that eight minutes, if she kept up this pace.

Nick could see Adele strutting from the car park and followed.
He really wanted to sprint, but a little voice inside his head
whispered that it would be better to let his wife cool off a bit.
He compromised by jogging.

Boy, she could walk fast when she took off like this. It was a minute or so before he gained enough ground to get within talking distance.

'Adele!'

She didn't even turn round, just held up a hand in his direction. The face obviously wasn't listening.

'Come on, Adele. Please?'

She had to stop at that moment to cross a road and he caught her up.

He started to open his mouth.

'Don't! Just don't,' she warned.

He shut it again.

'You've really outdone yourself this time, Nick. I can't believe you'd turn up here after nine months of no contact and invite me to a birthday party.' She laughed and shook her head. 'This is a new level of insensitivity, even for you.'

Now, hang on a minute! How many times had he called and tried to apologise in the days after he'd left? How many times had she slammed the receiver down before he'd been able to get more than a syllable out? If they hadn't communicated for nine months, it was more to do with Adele than it was with him. At least he'd tried.

In the end he'd done what she'd obviously wanted and let her be. And now she was blaming him for it?

'Well, maybe you've got all the answers, Adele, but I certainly haven't.'

She stepped back from the kerb and looked at him. 'What do you mean by that?'

'I mean, I'm not sure myself what is going on between us. What is this? Are we separated, or was it just a *really* long cooling-off period after a fight? If I can't figure it out, how am I supposed to define it for anyone else? You wouldn't talk to me. I have no idea what's going on in your neat and ordered little head.'

Adele shook her head and crossed the road. He had to wait

for a couple of cars to turn the corner before he could catch her up again. No more hanging around waiting for her to fill him in. He'd waited nine months and he was going to get his answers right now.

'What did you tell people, then, Adele? What was your take on it?'

And then he shut up. He knew exactly what Adele would have told her friends. Mona would have had every last grisly detail and would be in no doubt that Nick was the black-hearted villain of the piece, while Adele came off snowy white and smelling of roses. The woman was so blinkered some-times.

He marched along behind her in silence. He should have listened to his gut instinct. Adele was in no mood for even reasonable explanations. Anything he said would just make it worse while she was in this state.

While he waited for her to unlock the front door, the sparks flying off her were almost tangible.

'I'm going upstairs,' she said, and marched off, leaving the door open.

He stepped inside and closed it. Despite the twelve hours of sleep he'd had the night before, he was starting to flag again. He went into the living room and switched the televi-sion on. Maybe he could doze in front of it for a bit.

Adele would calm down soon enough. She always did. Her anger was quick to flare up, but it usually burnt itself out pretty quickly too. He flicked the television on and dropped into his favourite armchair. Just fifteen minutes watching the footie and he'd make her a cup of tea as a peace offering and see if they couldn't discuss things without world war three starting.

A little later, just as he was considering hauling himself out of his chair and switching the kettle on, he heard Adele coming down the stairs. Or, to be more precise, he heard a whole lot of bumping and crashing, then *thump, thump, thump*—as if there were two of her jumping down each step.

He arrived in the hall just in time to see Adele wrestling his bag down the last three stairs.

'Adele? What on earth are you doing?'

Adele stopped what she was doing, partly to answer, partly to catch her breath. Her arms were aching. How did a bunch of rumpled shirts weigh so much?

'I thought that was pretty obvious, wasn't it? I'm throwing you out.'

The look on his face was classic. If she weren't ready to kill him, she'd want to laugh. Finally, Nick Hughes had come across a woman who refused to melt at his feet and he was totally floored.

'You can't throw me out. I live here too.'

'Not any more. You can find some other poor sucker to rope into your hare-brained schemes. I'm finished with the whole lot of it.'

Her stomach dipped as she realised the implication of her own words. Was this really what four years of marriage had come to? She looked at Nick and the sickness sank right into her toes. That had wiped the dimples off his face. She should be feeling pleased he was finally getting the message, but suddenly she felt her eyes moisten.

'I'm sorry, Adele. Really I am. I should have told Mum…something.' He shook his head. 'But she loves you like a daughter and I didn't want to upset her. She's not very…'

He swallowed the rest of the sentence. She felt her heart squeeze as he struggled to find the words.

'She's been…I mean, going to be really sad for us. I didn't want to tell her until I knew for certain there wasn't any hope.'

No hope.

Her lip quivered and she pressed her mouth into a thin line to disguise it. Nick gave her a rueful smile. Now, this was the smile that *really* did some damage. It was heart-wrenchingly lopsided and utterly genuine.

The fault lines started to widen. Hadn't he said he didn't know how to define their relationship? Did that mean he hadn't made his mind up, that maybe he didn't want a divorce after all?

And, even if he did, why should she punish Maggie for her son's abandonment of his wife? Although there might not be a light at the end of the tunnel for her and Nick, she didn't want to cause bad feeling in the family.

She breathed in and out once, sharply. Family. For four years she'd been a part of a family and that had been wonderful. Phone calls on her birthday. Loud, overpopulated Sunday lunches with too much food and too little elbow room. The world was going to seem horribly empty when all that had gone for good.

She closed her eyes. No. She had to be strong. She couldn't weaken now. Missing out on one last chance to see them all—to say goodbye to them—was the price she'd have to pay to keep her sanity and her heart intact.

She had to focus on the fact that, once again, he was asking her to drop everything and trot off after him. And there were no guarantees that he wouldn't leave again after it was all over. He hadn't mentioned wanting to get back together again, had he? He just needed her to save his skin.

Too bad. He could save his own sorry hide.

He had no idea of the torment she'd been through after he'd left. She had to remember that black place and all the reasons why she never wanted to go back there.

So as Nick lounged against the door jamb, she let the blackness feed her anger until it was good and bubbling. And then she hauled his bag the short distance to the front door and flung it onto the garden path. When Nick let out a strangled *hey* and dived after it, she slammed the door and locked it behind him.

She punched the button on the remote control again and again. Celebrity chefs. TV's Worst Mishaps. Top Ten Pop Stars She Didn't Recognise. Why wasn't there anything good on the telly? She had more than fifty channels to choose from, for goodness' sake. There had to be something mildly interesting. Even a schmaltzy TV movie would be better than nothing.

Mind you, it *was* almost three o'clock in the morning.

She yawned. Normally she'd have been tucked up in bed hours ago, but tonight she just couldn't calm down enough even to bother with the pretence of going upstairs and getting changed into her PJs. And there was something oddly comforting about sitting in the dark with only the flicker of the television for company.

Mona would say she was wallowing. Mona would probably be right.

But a girl was allowed to wallow after she'd kicked the man she loved out of her life for good.

She threw the remote onto the sofa cushion next to her and tried to concentrate on the sitcom rerun she'd stopped at.

It was no good denying it. She loved Nick. He wouldn't make her half as crazy if she didn't. She might try to kid herself she was trying to lock him out of her heart as well as her house, but, in reality, there was no point. He was firmly embedded there.

But that didn't mean they were capable of building a life together.

They had different priorities. No, it was more than that. They were so utterly different that she wondered how things had lasted as long as four years. Five, if you counted the year before they got married. And then there was the year before that, when Nick had steadily pursued her and she had steadily refused until he'd worn her down and made her laugh.

She'd been very firm with him. One date—no more.

Only she'd discovered one date wasn't enough. Well, that was how it had seemed at the time. Maybe she'd have been better off listening to her feminine intuition—the alarm in her head that had yelled *code red, code red* every time Nick was in range.

She sighed and let her eyes wander round the room. It was stupid to feel so desolate at the thought of saying goodbye to Nick for ever. She'd made up her mind months ago.

The light on the answer-phone was blinking. Her heart hiccuped into action. Nick?

She jabbed the button and waited for the message.

'Hi, Nick. It's Debbie.'

Sister number two.

'Mum thought you might have got back by now. Hope the jet lag's not too bad. Anyway, just to let you know that Mum is over the worst of her last round of chemo, so it's all systems go for the party. Give me a ring and I'll fill you in. Tell Adele there's a chocolate torte with her name on it waiting for her. Bye.'

Chemo?

Nick's mum had cancer? The whole world seemed to somersault. Maggie couldn't die. She was too resilient, too vital. Why hadn't Nick told her?

Because you never gave him a chance, a little voice whispered. Too busy feeling sorry for yourself. You shut him out while you were grieving and then, when you were ready to listen, he'd given up. And she'd been too proud to call him, too battered and hurt to risk losing him again if he rejected her. She'd lost so much already. It had been easier to blame him and nurse her grief.

If only she could call him now. He must be feeling awful. But she'd slung him out without a thought as to where he might go and she had no idea how to contact him.

Whereas she had a few close friends she had known for years, Nick always seemed to have a nebulous cloud of acquaintances. He was popular, but he was always giving up one interest to try another, tiring of the same sports clubs and restaurants quickly.

The only one who'd been constant was his old college mate—what was his name? Kelvin? Connor? No, Callum. That was it. But she'd only met him twice and had no record of his address or phone number.

She sank back into the sofa and clicked the television off. The room was plunged into darkness, but she just sat there staring at nothing, for what seemed like hours.

Then she heard a rattle at the front door. She held her breath. It must be the wind, surely? She strained to hear more but it had all gone quiet again. The door had two locks, anyway. She was just about to breathe out when she heard the noise again.

No. This time it wasn't just a rattle. She could hear the lock turning. Goose-pimples broke out all over her arms and her stomach nosedived, but somehow she couldn't move. All she could do was huddle herself into a ball in the corner of the sofa and try to slow the rise and fall of her chest.

If only Nick were here! Why couldn't this have happened last night when the big lunk had been asleep in the kitchen?

Then came the sound she had been dreading: the second lock clicked and she heard the door creak open. She held her breath and, as quietly as she could, she eased herself off the sofa and hid behind the armchair. Her ankles cracked as she crouched down and she was sure the noise was as loud as a gunshot.

Someone was in the house! She began to shake. The phone. She needed the phone.

But it was across the other side of the room, and the intruder was moving down the hall towards the living-room door. She couldn't risk it. Even if she could creep over there and make it back in time, she'd be heard talking once she made the call.

She peered out over the arm of the chair just as the living-room door brushed across the carpet. A shadow moved towards her and she froze.

CHAPTER THREE

THE burglar felt down the side of the armchair. He was so close his breath warmed the air near her. He didn't find what he was looking for and moved his arm to reach behind the side of the chair where she was hiding.

Adele did the only thing she could think of. He wasn't wearing gloves and when his hand was only inches from her face she lunged forward and sank her teeth into the exposed skin of his wrist.

He let out a yelp of pain and jumped back, tripping over his own feet as he did so.

'What the…?'

Adele had been preparing to scratch and bite and kick and do anything she could think of to get out of there safely. Her leg was draped across the arm of the chair, ready to spring over it and out of the door while he was off balance.

The hairs on the back of her neck rose. That voice…

'Nick?'

There was a shuffling noise as he got to his feet.

'Thanks for the warm welcome, sweetheart!'

'What are you…? What do you think you…?' The adrenaline surge quickly converted fear to anger. Given a choice of fight or flight, Adele was ready to get down and dirty. However, the heightened state of awareness seemed to be short-circuiting her ability to form a coherent sentence.

She closed her eyes, took a deep breath and tried again.

'What the heck are you doing creeping round my house in the middle of the night?'

'*Our* house.'

'Stop nit-picking! You scared me half to death!'

'I was looking for—' Nick leaned over and turned on a table lamp '—this.'

He reached past her and picked up a leather wallet lying by her foot.

'And this.'

A mobile phone was only a few inches away.

Adele stared at it. It wasn't the one he'd used to have. For some strange reason the knowledge made her very sad.

'I took them out of my jeans pocket earlier on. I discovered that it's actually very hard to find somewhere to stay with none of my friends' phone numbers and no money for a hotel.'

She was so dazed she didn't know what to say. One minute she'd been wishing him here and, now her wish had been granted, she was ready to boot him out of the door again. All her anger suffocated in a cloud of bafflement.

'How did you get in?' she asked, still staring at the phone.

Nick reached into his back pocket, pulled out a set of keys and dangled them from the tip of his finger. Adele focused on them slowly.

He shrugged. 'I thought you'd be in bed. I'd planned to slip in quietly, get my things and disappear again. You would never have known I'd been here.'

'You have keys?' Why were the most basic concepts so hard to grasp all of a sudden?

'Yup.'

She tightened her forehead until her brows puckered. 'So,

if you still have keys, why didn't you use them when you first turned up here?'

'Dunno. I was trying to be polite, I suppose.'

Nick? Trying to be polite? Did not compute.

He'd dive-bombed into her life again in his size-eleven boots, tried to manoeuvre her into going to a party five hundred miles away and he was worried about letting himself into his own house? It was so absurd she couldn't even start to get her head round it.

So she did the only thing she could; she collapsed into the chair, one leg hanging over the edge, and started to laugh. And then she found she couldn't stop. Pretty soon, tears were running down her face.

Only Nick could do this. The man was impossible, intolerable and impossible some more.

For once, Nick didn't have a cheeky grin plastered all over his face. He just kept staring at her and blinking. He looked so lost, and when he looked like that he was impossible to resist.

She let the rest of the mirth out on one long breath and shook her head. 'You'll never find anywhere to stay at this time of night. You might as well go and get your things and put them in the spare room. We'll talk later.'

When Adele swept into the kitchen at six-thirty that morning she found Nick sitting at the table waiting for her. She stopped in her tracks and tilted her head to one side.

'You're up early.' About three hours too early for his normal routine.

'You said we were going to talk.'

She pushed up the stiff cuff of her blouse and looked at her watch. 'I'm not missing work today, Nick. I have a life and I'm not putting it on hold for you.'

He grimaced. 'Yeah, and don't I know it.'

'What's that supposed to mean?'

He rubbed the corner of one eye with his index finger. 'Ignore me. I'm tired and grumpy. The rest of us mortals don't spring out of bed before dawn without a hair out of place like you do.'

He might not be dressed, but he was looking much better than mortal with his pyjamas done up on the wrong button and his hair sticking up in five different directions.

Hold on. Since when did Nick wear pyjamas?

But then her thoughts veered dangerously to what he normally wore in bed and a blush crept up her neck and kept going until it was under her hairline. Pyjamas were definitely better for her blood pressure than the alternative.

Adele looked down at her skirt and blouse and her high heels then smoothed an invisible hair into the twist at the back of her head.

He'd done it again. Sometimes, all Nick had to do was be in the same room as her and she was questioning herself. When she'd walked down the stairs this morning she'd felt confident, efficient, ready to face the world. Now she just felt…overdressed.

'I'm just up and ready for the office, that's all. Some of us can't spend all our time locked in the garden shed until three in the morning and call it work, you know.'

Nick yawned and covered his hand with his mouth. 'I'm too tired to have this argument again. Can we just take it as a given that I act like a three-year-old and you're the grown-up? Then we can skip all the shouting.'

She wanted to say 'No, I don't want to skip it,' but that would make *her* the three-year-old, so she bit her tongue and made her way to the coffee-maker. Much to her surprise, it was already on and hot, steaming coffee was waiting for her.

Nick got up from where he was sitting and handed her a mug.

'The office doesn't open until nine. We've got time to talk.'

Adele opened her mouth to speak.

'Yes, I know you always like to be in before eight, but even then we've got time.'

She closed it again and nodded. However, once she and Nick were seated either side of the table again, the room fell into silence.

Finally, Adele could bear it no more.

'Why didn't you tell me your mum was ill?'

Nick's jaw dropped. 'How did you find out?'

'Debbie left a message for you on the answer-phone. I suppose your mum's not the only one who doesn't know we've been living apart for almost a year.'

'You know how close they all are. If any of them knew, they'd be sure to blab it to Mum and I didn't want to give her the extra worry.'

'You should have told me.'

Nick gave her a lopsided look. 'I seem to remember hearing an awful lot of dial tone in our phone conversations.'

'Not then. Now. Why didn't you say anything yesterday?'

'It seemed too much like emotional blackmail.'

She took a sip of her coffee. 'I would call it being honest, actually.'

'Are you telling me that you wouldn't have felt duty bound to make the trip, even if it was the last thing on earth you wanted to do?'

She looked down and rubbed at a mark on the table with her fingertip. Nick was right. She would have gone to the party whether she wanted to or not if she'd known the truth. The thought didn't sit comfortably with her. In her opinion, knowing all the facts meant she was in control. She wasn't going to let him use keeping her in the dark as an excuse, even if, by some strange logic, it sounded kind of noble.

'Well, I know now, don't I?'

Nick's smile didn't reach his eyes. 'What are you going to do?'

She breathed in and sat up straight. 'I propose we deal with this in an adult manner. I'll go to Scotland with you. I love your mum and I wouldn't want to upset her, but—'

Nick leapt up from where he was sitting and hauled her into his arms.

'Thank you,' he whispered into her ear. 'I really mean it. This is going to mean so much to Mum. You don't know how grateful I am.'

She would have told him how much she understood if he hadn't been squeezing her so tight she thought her lungs would collapse. So much for dealing with this in an adult manner.

Her hands made contact with his shoulders and she was going to prise herself from the hug, but then the smell of him, the warm feeling from his arms around her started to work on her senses. It had been so long since she'd hugged anyone.

In fact, she didn't think she'd had a proper cuddle since Nick had left. Mona didn't do mushy stuff, as she put it. That left baby Bethany and her older brother, Josh. But even those hugs were bitter-sweet, reminding her of what could have been, but now never would be.

She told herself to let go, to ease herself out of his arms now his grip was loosening, but he smelled so good and felt so warm that she had to hang on for a couple more seconds. And then a few seconds more.

Slowly, she became aware that the hands that had been squeezing were now flat against her back. The fingers started to move, softly stroking, and a shiver skipped up her spine and kept travelling upwards until the tingle concentrated somewhere behind her ears.

Then she heard him inhale, as if he were breathing in her scent and couldn't get enough of it, and it tipped her completely over the edge. Moisture welled in her eyes and collected in her lower lashes.

She yearned for the days of blissful ignorance when she'd thought they'd last for ever. She missed the knowledge in that, in at least one person's eyes, she was special, good enough. It was such a pity that reality had eventually had to intrude on the fantasy.

He pulled back to look at her and she saw an answering ache in his eyes.

'Adele,' he whispered as he lowered his head.

She meant to duck away from the kiss, but somehow she couldn't. She was trapped by a magnetic force that kept her clinging to him. Maybe it was a trick of memory, or maybe it was because she'd been unknowingly waiting for this moment for the last nine months, but this kiss was even better than the ones she tried not to remember, more electrically charged, more tender, more sweet, more…everything.

It was only as her fingers wandered to the top button of his skew-whiff pyjamas that she came to her senses. What was she doing? Was she mad?

She mustn't forget that when she'd faced the worst crisis of her life, he'd abandoned her. She hadn't been able to depend on him. No matter how much they cared for each other or how good the chemistry was, it didn't mean they could survive a future together without tearing each other into tiny shreds.

She left the button in its proper place and scrabbled away from him.

He reached for her and she shook her head. 'This changes nothing.'

In fact, it had. It made the path she had to take even clearer. If she were to keep her heart safe from this man, she was going to have to take drastic measures. She slipped into business-mode, all starch and crisp efficiency. It was the only way to get through this.

'As I said, I propose we deal with this in an adult manner, no matter how daft it is that you've been keeping your mum in the dark.'

Nick's smile wavered altogether. 'I was trying to save her extra stress at a time when she already had enough on her plate. Breast cancer is pretty serious, you know. I wouldn't call what I did juvenile.'

Inwardly Adele squirmed, but she didn't twitch a millimetre on the outside. Not even an eyelash. She made very sure of that.

'I know cancer is serious. I'm not stupid. I'm just saying you went about this in entirely the wrong way. You just bounded in like you always do and played the situation from moment to moment, rather than considering what the long-term consequences would be. You have to tell her the truth about us.'

'What is the truth, Adele? One minute you're pushing me away, the next you're… What happened just now, for instance?'

She shuffled backwards until her bottom bumped against the counter. 'That was you getting over-enthusiastic, as usual.'

The wary look in his eyes said he wasn't buying it completely. So what? Neither was she, but that didn't mean she was going to cave in and admit it.

'You make me sound like a Labrador.'

Adele swallowed. She hadn't meant to insult him, only keep him at arm's length the best way she knew how—with words. Sharp, nasty, barbed-wire words.

And the truth was, at his best, he was like a Labrador— loyal, loving and with boundless energy, but that didn't make him any less destructive, and she had more at stake than a pair of soggy slippers or a chewed newspaper.

'And you seemed fairly enthusiastic yourself,' he added.

He was right. How pathetic had she been? She'd spent

almost a year carefully building up her defences against him and he'd turned them to marshmallow in just over twenty-four hours.

She had to do something to safeguard herself, to make sure the barbed wire was nailed firmly in place.

'You want an answer from me about where this relationship is going?'

He threw his hands up, asking a question. 'I was hoping that we'd have a chance to work that one out on the drive to Invergarrig.'

'You don't have to wait for the weekend; I can tell you now.'

Nick just stared at her.

'I'll go to the party with you, Nick, but there are some conditions.'

'Conditions,' he echoed.

'Yes. It's time you stopped stampeding over other people's lives. It's time to take responsibility for your actions.'

His mouth thinned into a line, but while he wasn't answering back or flashing his dimples she needed to forge on.

'I will do you this favour if you agree to a divorce. When we get home from Scotland, I'm going to see a solicitor.'

He couldn't have looked more stunned if she'd actually reached out and slapped him round the face. Her stomach lurched as she heard her own words echo in her ears.

There. She'd said it out loud; she couldn't undo it now.

'It's time to move on. I've got a life of my own to lead. I can't spend the rest of it clearing up after you.'

Nick looked her straight in the eye and this time she did squirm. He seemed greyer, with all the boundless energy sucked out of him.

'Fine. At least I know where I stand now.'

The sticky edge of the envelope refused to behave itself. Even when Nick had finished trying to smooth it down it was still bumpy and slightly off to one side. He propped it up against the coffee-maker—Adele's first stop after a busy day at the office.

His bag was waiting for him in the hall, standing guard almost. He picked it up, hauled it outside and closed the door gently behind him. Then he stared at the glossy black paint on the front door for a good ten seconds.

The keys were warm when he pulled them from his back pocket. The letterbox felt icy in comparison, still cold from the overnight frost. He pushed against the stiff flap and dropped the bunch of keys inside. When he heard them jangle against the mat, he turned and walked away.

The air seemed curiously still when Adele opened the front door and dropped her briefcase in its usual spot. She tried to work out what was missing as she wrestled herself free of her coat and hung it away in the cupboard.

Nick must be in his workshop, rummaging for his famous recipe for fake blood. She'd make them a nice dinner and they'd discuss the situation calmly and rationally. They just didn't work well together as a couple, that was all. There was no reason why the separation couldn't be amicable. They could still be friends.

The envelope was the first thing she saw as she walked into the kitchen. She frowned. Nick's handwriting in bright green felt-tip.

She picked it up and opened it, using her index finger as a paper knife, and pulled out a couple of thin sheets torn from a ring-bound notepad.

Adele, I'm staying at Craig's for a couple of nights— thought it was best we both had a bit of space. Mum would like us to be up in Invergarrig on Friday night for a family dinner. Let me know if that's not convenient

*and we'll travel up on Saturday instead. I'll give you
a call in a couple of days when we've both had a chance
to cool down.*
N

Cool down? She was perfectly cool!

She folded the sheets in half, even smoothing down the
frilly edges where they had been torn from the notepad, and
placed them back inside the envelope. Then she didn't know
what to do with it, so she propped it up against the coffee-
maker again and walked out of the kitchen.

She made her way upstairs and absent-mindedly turned on
the bath taps.

Who the hell was Craig, anyway?

She got undressed and left her clothes in an uncharacteristic heap on the floor and tried to let the hot water wash away
her disappointment. It was the coward's way out—leaving a
note like that. She should know.

She leaned forward and twisted the hot tap until the water
splashing into the bath was just short of scalding.

At least she'd had a proper reason for not being able to face
Nick last May. Leaving a note might have been gutless, but
it had been all she could manage at the time.

Why was he so surprised at her request for a divorce?
They hadn't been living together—hadn't even spoken—for
months. What did he think was going to happen?

Since the bath was threatening to overflow, she reached
forward and turned off the taps. Then she sank back into the
blissfully hot water and tried to loosen her shoulder muscles.

She scrubbed her face and tried not to notice the way every
sound echoed round the bathroom. Echoed round the house,
even. It had taken her months to get used to living alone.

She'd only ever envisaged their Victorian terraced house
as a nest for her and Nick, somewhere they could be impos-

sibly happy and gradually fill with children. When he'd disappeared, taking the possibility of all that with him, she hadn't
been able to stand being there any more. Too many daydreams burst like balloons.

All she'd wanted was a home that seemed warm and
inviting, a place you could walk into and feel the love. She
and Nick had spent a couple of years doing it up, but now it
didn't seem to matter if they'd got just the right door knobs
for the kitchen cabinets. A home was more than furniture and
fixtures. Of all people, she should know that.

Her own family home had been a suburban palace, fitting
for the business king who owned it. Pity it hadn't been designed with children in mind. 'Don't touch' and 'Look what
you've done!' had seemed to echo round the high-ceilinged
rooms. Her mother had been forty-one when she'd had her—
a complete shock by all accounts. Adele suspected her mother
had never quite got over it.

She'd certainly never let the existence of a daughter slow
her down. She'd hired a nanny and continued to travel the
world with her husband. To Adele she'd always seemed a little
far-off and glamorous—a bit like the queen.

Adele rested her head on the bath and stared at the ceiling.

She'd had such great plans for this house—for her life—
and, in one swift move, Nick had turned everything upside
down.

When he'd left she'd tried to give it a new identity. A few
new prints on the walls, different pot plants in the living
room.

Of course, she'd cleared up all his things and stuck them
in a box in the wardrobe almost immediately she'd returned
from her stay at Mona's, but the lingering stamp of Nick on
the house had been harder to erase.

Eventually she'd managed to stop expecting to find his
jacket slung over the back of the sofa, or to have to close the

back door he'd left open after racing down to his workshop to try out his latest brainwave.

He'd only been back a couple of days and now she had to start all over again. And it wasn't as if his stuff was scattered round the house this time. No, this time it was all in her head, and she wasn't sure she had the energy to spring clean it right at the moment, not when she had to spend the weekend with him. Better save it for Monday.

She wouldn't tell Mona, though. Mona would get the wrong idea and think she didn't mean what she said about the divorce.

Nick stayed true to his word—he didn't phone for a few days. That didn't stop Adele jumping out of her skin every time she heard it ring. In the end, she decided to let the answer-phone save her from any more breathless *hellos*. It was getting embarrassing.

Then, on Wednesday night, at eight forty-three, she heard his voice on the speaker and froze.

'Adele? It's me. I…um…we need to decide what time we want to leave on Friday morning.' There was a long pause. 'I'll call again later and see if I can catch you in.' Five seconds passed—Adele knew because she counted them in elephants—and then he hung up.

She carefully slid her laptop off her thighs and onto the sofa and walked over to the phone. The caller ID revealed a number she didn't recognise. The accommodating Craig's, she guessed.

She pressed the dial button and waited while it rang.

'Hello?'

The voice was young, blonde and was still halfway through a giggle. Adele stiffened.

'Could I speak with Nick, please?'

'Sure. He's just in the other room.' There were muffled

noises as the girl covered the mouthpiece with her hand. She didn't do a very good job of it, because Adele still heard everything she said.

'Nicky?' she yelled. 'It's for you…I think it's your mum.'

Nicky? Adele shuddered. And she wasn't even going to think about the other comment.

She could hear him laughing as he made his way to the phone and held her breath as he picked it up.

'I'm wearing my clean underwear just in case I get run over by a bus, Mum, I promise.'

'Bully for you.'

'Adele!'

'Craig sounds a lot blonder and squeakier than I thought he would.'

'Huh? Oh, no. That's Kai. She's his girlfriend—this week. How did you know she was blonde?'

Adele rolled her eyes. 'Lucky guess.'

'I take it you heard my message.'

'Yes.'

'So, are we going up Friday or Saturday?'

She bit her lip. An extra day with Nick was going to be difficult, but it might be the last time she got to see her in-laws. A family dinner sounded wonderful.

'I can do Friday.'

She heard him exhale. 'That's great. We're going to have to leave early, though.'

'How early?'

'Dunno. Haven't settled on a time yet.'

Typical. He hadn't thought about this at all.

'Well, what time is the dinner?'

'Hang on a second—Mum rang me with all the details. I just need to find them.'

The phone at his end clattered onto a hard surface and she heard a rustling noise. It must have driven Maggie mad not to send him a little card with all the details in it, just in case he forgot. Honestly, she'd put little notes in his packed-lunch box if she could.

'OK,' he said, sounding slightly breathless. 'It starts at eight.'

'Let's aim to get there for six at the latest. It should give us a bit of time to stretch our legs and freshen up. How long will it take us?'

'Debbie says it takes her nine hours, but she's about an hour closer, so I'd suggest we leave at eight.'

'Let's make it seven. We've got the M25 to deal with.'

Nick groaned.

'What time are you picking me up, then?' Adele asked.

Silence for a few seconds.

'You've got the car, Adele. I didn't sneak one back into the country in my hand luggage, you know.'

Adele closed her eyes and dropped onto the sofa. 'So, not only am I going to be stuck in a car with you for eleven hours, I'm going to have to do the driving as well?'

'We can share. I'll let you do the first leg.'

'Gee, thanks.' She opened her eyes and gave the ceiling a long, hard look. 'You'd better tell me Craig's address. I want you standing on the doorstep at seven o'clock sharp or I'm driving away without you.'

Now who was sounding like his mother?

'Whatever you say.'

Adele just knew he was doing a little cocky smirk at the phone. Her lips curled into a smile anyway.

Impossible. The man was impossible.

If it weren't the crack of dawn, Adele would've been leaning on the horn with all her weight. It was bad enough she'd ended up as chauffeur, without being made to wait around in her car in sub-zero temperatures. The heater was a bit dodgy and would only produce something approaching warmth once her foot was near the floor.

The clock on the dashboard ticked. Seven minutes past seven. He had until ten past and then she was aborting the mission.

She shook her head. Aborting the mission. What kind of phrase was that? She was starting to sound more and more like Mona with each passing day. Anyone would think this was some kind of military operation.

Adele jabbed the radio on with a gloved finger.

Maybe she was on to something.

Maybe if she treated this like a campaign she might emerge, if not triumphant, at least with her heart and her dignity intact. She couldn't let Nick worm his way past her defences this time. If she failed, and had to pick up the pieces afterwards, there wouldn't be enough bits left over to glue back together to make a whole Adele. She'd never be the same.

The only problem was she knew nothing about warfare. Only a few jumbled phrases from World War Two movies and things her rather stern grandfather had used to say.

Know your enemy.

Well, that was easy enough. She knew Nick inside out. Didn't help much, though. The more she thought about him the more she seemed to turn to mush. And this soldier wasn't going to do mush, thank you very much.

Always keep the element of surprise.

Adele smiled and stroked the steering wheel, a smile widening across her cheeks. Nick was going to go mad when he saw the car. She smothered a giggle with her hand and the fluff of the angora glove tickled her lips.

It was about time Nick had a taste of his own medicine. She rubbed her hands together. So, this was what it felt like to be bad. The scary thing was, it felt kind of good.

The second hand of the clock juddered towards the twelve.

It was nine minutes past seven…and forty seconds…and forty-five seconds. Adele turned the key in the ignition.

True to form, Nick burst from the front door of the flat with a holdall and a small backpack. He hadn't spotted her yet. A stocky guy with red hair handed Nick what looked like a sports bag. Nick clapped him on the back and smiled.

Then the smile dropped off Adele's face. Something blonde and skinny ran from inside, flung its arms round Nick's neck and plastered a big kiss on his cheek. Adele growled then suddenly stopped, surprised at herself.

A few seconds later her soon-to-be-ex-husband was down the garden path and looking up and down the street. Adele wound down her window and waved. Nick waved back—and then did a double-take.

She grimaced. He was striding this way and he didn't look very happy.

'Adele! What have you done with the car?'

'Shhh! It's seven o'clock in the morning.'

'I know what blooming time it is. I want to know what you've done with my car!'

'Our car—and I sold it.'

'You…you…' He looked heavenwards then pressed his lips together and shook his head. She flinched as he opened the boot and threw his bags inside. One of them jangled, which was a bit odd, but she didn't stop to think about it. She had more pressing matters holding her attention.

Nick got in the passenger seat, slammed the door closed and turned to face her.

'Well?'

'We didn't need that boxy old thing any more. It's not practical for the city.'

Nick seemed to be mouthing the words *boxy old thing*.

She swallowed. Perhaps she'd gone a bit too far.

Selling their Jeep had been the only bit of revenge she'd

had. She'd wanted to shred his shirts to ribbons with a razor blade, but she just hadn't been able to bring herself to do it. They'd still smelled of him.

'I needed something smaller, more efficient—a little runabout.'

He poked at a button on the dashboard. Nothing happened.

'A little rust bucket, more like,' he muttered. 'If this is all you got for the money you should have got from my Jeep, then you were well and truly done.'

She gave him a sideways glance. 'I'm not stupid. I didn't spend all of the money on this. I'm perfectly capable of buying a car without your input, you know.'

He snorted. 'Adele, *capable* is your middle name. Why would I ever think you needed me for anything?'

'Now you're just being ridiculous.'

Nick turned away to do up his seat belt.

Adele followed suit. 'I suppose you'd like me to be a bit more like blondie over there, falling all over you and worshipping at your feet? Does she always wander round in just a vest top and a pair of knickers? She must be very resilient to the cold.'

Nick's lips stayed firmly clamped together as he smiled. 'She's from Sweden. She's used to it.'

Adele crunched the gear stick into place and checked the rear-view mirror, scowling.

'Of course, sometimes she forgets to wear the vest,' he added.

She yanked at the handbrake.

Nick chuckled. 'I'm kidding, Adele. Lighten up. We've got a long journey ahead. I thought we could stop in the Midlands around lunchtime. Let's make nice, polite conversation until then.'

'You do the talking. I'm driving.'

'OK. Now, what shall we talk about? I know. Going back

to our earlier conversation, there was at least *one* thing you needed me for. Begged me for on occasion, if I recall rightly.'

Adele hunched over the steering wheel and said nothing. At this rate, Nick would be lucky if he was still alive by lunchtime.

CHAPTER FOUR

A LORRY hulked past in the outside lane and Adele gripped the steering wheel a little tighter. What was it about being over-taken by one of those monsters that made you sure you were going to veer off the road and end up in a heap of twisted metal?

Nick was fumbling in the rucksack at his feet. She flicked a look over and breathed a sigh of relief. He had one of his gadgets in his hand—probably his iPod—and she'd have a few moments' peace if he plugged himself in.

Much to her annoyance he started fixing a big sucker with an arm attached to the windscreen.

'What on earth are you up to now?'

Nick just grinned. 'Just wait and see. You'll love it.'

Another truck decided to overtake with millimetres to spare and she fixed her eyes on the motorway lane in front of her. When she had a chance to look again, Nick was huddled over the gadget, pressing buttons in rapid succession. It beeped back at him. He reached over and fixed it into the cradle stuck to the windscreen.

'Satellite navigation,' he said proudly.

She rolled her eyes then concentrated on keeping well back from the car in front.

'I should have guessed that eventually you would get a

whole host of gizmos to do your thinking for you, especially now I'm not around.'

'You're sitting right next to me. You are around.'

'You know what I mean. You're a typical man. God forbid you actually pick up the road atlas.'

'Adele, you would never let me within ten feet of the road atlas. Admit it, sweetheart, you just don't like giving up the control.'

'So not true. I just like having something to do on long journeys.'

And she'd been looking for a distraction, something to take her mind off the man sitting so close to her that all her nerve-endings were sizzling with awareness and she was constantly on edge.

Come on, who liked being replaced by a machine? She glared at the contraption as it sat in its cradle.

'What happens if that thing gets you hopelessly lost?'

Nick leaned back and stretched his legs out. 'Impossible. That's the beauty of it. The information is always at your fin-gertips. It pinpoints exactly where you are, night and day.'

She stopped glaring and studied the display. Maybe she should give it a go?

'It never goes wrong?'

Nick shrugged. 'It's a machine. It has its moments but, on the whole, it's as accurate as you would be. Just about perfect.'

Adele sighed. Perfect. How she was learning to hate that word.

She knew all about the pressures of having to be right one hundred per cent of the time, of having everyone expecting you to be perfect. No, not just expecting—relying on you being perfect. It was such a strain to have to juggle everything and never having the luxury of knowing that, if you dropped a ball once in a while, it didn't matter.

The rattle from the engine warned her that her foot had been heavier on the accelerator than she had intended. Eighty-five? Whoops. She carefully eased off the pedal.

A cut-glass, metallic voice pierced the silence. *'In nine hundred feet, take the next exit.'*

Adele squinted at the display, but the sun was on it and she couldn't see it properly.

'That means get over into the other lane, Adele. We're going to miss the exit if you don't.'

Easier said than done. Half the traffic on the motorway was trying to leave by that exit and there wasn't a space to slip into. She tried to find a gap without causing a pile-up, but there were too many cars all packed too closely together.

'Take the next exit. Take the next exit.'

By the time she had checked her mirrors again and tried to slow down, it was too late. The rust bucket sailed right past the cluttered slip-road.

Nick threw his hands in the air. 'Great!'

She glared at him. 'It would have been easier if you'd just let me rely on my own eyes and ears and read the signs! I'm not used to using this stupid—'

The sat nav interrupted her with a persistent binging noise. A huge question mark flashed on its screen. *'Perform an U-turn as soon as possible,'* it ordered in an infuriatingly calm manner.

'Be quiet, you bossy woman!' she yelled back. 'We're on a motorway. I thought *you* were supposed to know that!'

Nick threw his head back and roared with laughter.

Of course, he would find it funny.

The service station was a welcome sight, although not the most glamorous of locations. Adele leapt out of the car and headed for the Ladies'. Once there, she placed her hands on the shelf in front of a wide mirror and leaned forward to let them take her weight.

She breathed out and stared at herself. Her hair was still in its pony-tail and she looked as neat and tidy as always, but as she studied her reflection she could tell she was coming slightly unravelled. It was something about her eyes, a slight downturn of her mouth.

She stared until she thought she would go cross-eyed and then she straightened, pulled her shoulders back and lifted her chin.

It was a familiar routine. One she'd learned at school when she needed to present a brave face to the world. She hadn't had the charm and easy wit of some of her classmates, but what she'd lacked in confidence she'd made up for with observation and hard work.

She'd spent hours studying the popular girls, the way they stood and talked. Even their laughs and hand gestures. Then she'd got up early and practised in the bathroom mirror while everyone else was snoring. Pretty soon she'd had friends and the teachers seemed to notice her more and, by the end of her days at Lumley College, she'd been head girl.

No one need know the geeky girl still lurked under the surface. She was hidden by the right body language, a certain glint in the eyes. It was like slipping on a cloak, an outer skin that nobody bothered to look beneath.

She could normally make the transformation with a single bat of her eyelashes, but today had been especially trying and she needed the reassurance the mirror could give her.

Over the years her alter ego had spent more and more time in the limelight. Nowadays the real Adele only peeked out when safely within the sanctuary of her own home. Maybe one day the shy little girl would get drowned out by this alternate persona altogether and the brisk efficiency, the confidence, would be real.

She smiled. Eventually she'd named the other side of her personality. Super Adele she'd called her. Only instead of a cape and unforgiving Lycra, her costume had more to do with the way she held herself, the smile gauged to be just bright enough without being obviously fake. The precise dimensions had taken years to perfect.

Carefully, she added another layer of mascara and brushed the lipstick across her lips. There. Ready to face the world—on the outside, anyway.

She hoisted her handbag squarely back onto her shoulder and walked over to the door.

Super Adele had seemed such a good idea in the beginning. Everybody loved her. And, for a while, she'd revelled in the attention. Nowadays, the adoration had lost its warm glow.

It's her they love, not me.

Even Nick. He'd fallen in love with Super Adele.

When they'd first been married, she'd gloried in the way he'd thought she could do anything, be anything, but after a couple of years it had just got tiring. She'd tried to climb down off the pedestal, but Nick wouldn't let her. He was holding fast to Super Adele and wasn't going to let her go.

The impulse to sag and let her shoulders droop was almost overwhelming, but she straightened her spine further. The restaurant was just in front of her and she could see Nick sitting at a table waiting for her.

Oh, how she longed to just slump into the moulded plastic seat, lay her head on the table and sob.

Sometimes she hated her alter ego.

Nick let Adele sweep off and made his way to the café. An abundance of bright plastic and the smell of greasy food greeted him. He avoided the ageing sausages and other offerings—they looked as if they had been sitting under the heat lamps for at least a week—and bought two cups of grim-looking coffee instead.

He settled into an off-white seat near the streaky windows that filled one side of the room and waited for Adele to appear.

The restaurant was practically deserted. An elderly couple were working their way through a rubbery-looking fried breakfast with excruciating slowness, a businessman took refuge behind a crisp newspaper and a teenager in a dirty apron was only just pretending to clean the tables.

She soon appeared and sat down, all stiff and starchy, in the seat opposite him. He hated it when she did that. She didn't need to put on a front with him.

'Come on, Adele. It's not the end of the world. It didn't take us long to find the next exit and work our way back to the right motorway.'

Adele nodded and sipped her coffee. As always, her anger had run out of fuel and she was left feeling drained.

He caught her eye. 'Have you ever maybe thought that your standards are a little too high? You set yourself punishing goals and are tough on yourself if you don't achieve them. You don't have to prove yourself over and over, you know. It was just a wrong turning. Everybody goes the wrong way at one time or another.'

'I'm not trying to prove anything or impress anyone. I just like things to be done right. I only ask of myself what I expect in others. It would be hypocritical if I didn't.'

He nodded slightly to himself. Talk about hitting the nail on the head. To live up to Adele's standards you needed to be able to pole-vault.

'I think the closer people get to you, the higher the pass mark is.'

'Don't be silly. People don't need to sit an exam to be my friends.'

Oh, no? Then why did he feel as if every word, every movement he made was being weighed and judged?

'I think you want everyone to do things the way you do.'

She shook her head while she swallowed a sip of coffee.

'Just because I don't plan everything a year in advance, it

doesn't mean I'm hopeless,' he continued. 'I'm different from you, Adele, but that doesn't mean I don't get things done or I don't care. I do. I've never missed a deadline or broken a contract. It might look like I'm winging it to you, but I'm not. We just have different methods for achieving our goals.'

'I know that.'

He wanted to hold his stomach and laugh out loud until the retired couple gave him dirty looks.

This was pointless. If he couldn't make her see sense, he might as well settle for improving her mood. He should have got a little gold star for resisting the urge to crack a joke and try and force a smile out of her.

'Do you want a *pain au chocolat*? I saw some on the counter.'

She nodded again, a hint of a smile on her face. He jumped up and paid for it quickly. If Adele didn't get a blood-sugar boost soon, she'd never cheer up.

He tipped his head to one side and took a good look at her. 'You look wiped out.'

'Thanks a lot.'

He reached forward and took her hand. She looked tired, all the fight sucked out of her, but she was still incredibly beautiful. Not in a showy way, but there was a strength in her delicate features that gave an indication of her drive and tenacity, an intelligent light behind her eyes that warned him to keep on his toes.

'I'll drive the next leg. Are you insured for that?'

Just for a nanosecond, she visibly sagged. 'It's me, Nick. Of course I'm insured. For everything—flood, fire, acts of God, spontaneous combustion… Go on, make a joke about that.'

He squeezed her hand. He'd always loved her fingers—long and fine. He'd missed them.

'You go back to the car and sink into the passenger seat. I've got a couple of things to get from the shop.'

He watched her as she walked away. She always stood so straight, so proud.

How he was going to demolish those proud barriers, he didn't know. But one thing was certain: he wanted his wife back, and he was going to do everything in his power this weekend to remind her how much she wanted him too.

Just as well he had a few tricks up his sleeve to help nudge her in the right direction.

Pretending to be asleep could in fact be very tiring, Adele decided. She twitched open an eyelid and took a sideways look at Nick. Look at him humming to himself and acting as if he didn't have a care in the world.

Only a few days ago she'd told this man she wanted him out of her life for good. Yes, he'd looked a little angry at the time, but now it didn't seem as if it bothered him at all.

She relaxed her eyelid and it dropped closed.

She wasn't a vindictive person, but part of her was really upset that *he* wasn't more upset. Deciding to walk away from their marriage had been the hardest decision of her life. She wanted Nick to look at least a little shell-shocked.

A huge sigh juddered from her body.

For a person who had a pathological need to be right, she wasn't taking much joy in the fact that, once again, her instincts had been spot-on. Nick didn't take her seriously, didn't take their marriage seriously. If he had, he wouldn't be so blasé about the whole thing.

Then again, if he'd cared, he wouldn't have left in the first place. He might say he loved her, but he didn't love her enough. The job had meant more to him.

But now he was back, looking all delectable. And he'd kissed her in the kitchen, hadn't he? Was there a possibility that he'd regretted his decision to abandon her?

When she'd stood at the front of the church with him, and

they'd exchanged their vows, she'd thought it was going to last for ever. She'd been swept along by the intense chemistry between them and hadn't even stopped to question if there had been enough there to sustain a fifty-year relationship. It had just seemed as if all the right ingredients were there and she hadn't bothered to dig any deeper.

He'd made her believe they were two contrasting halves of the same whole. Sweet and sour. Light and dark. But, in the end, it had turned out that they were just too different. More like oil and water.

The analogy just didn't hold up. As soon as the sun arrived, night was swallowed up and it was daytime again. They couldn't co-exist without one destroying the other—and neither could she and Nick.

A voice she was learning to hate cut the silence. *'In one thousand feet, take the next exit.'*

She opened her eyes and sat up. They were leaving the motorway already? Had she really been asleep and missed most of the journey? A crazy flame of relief flickered in her chest.

It was raining, but instead of the craggy hills and pine trees she'd expected to see, there were rolling fields and hedgerows. And the landscape was depressingly flat. It all looked far too English.

'Why are we coming off the motorway, Nick? Where are we?'

'Somewhere just outside of Stafford. Pit stop,' he added by way of explanation.

Despite the empty feeling in her tummy, she felt her taste buds rebel at the thought of more plastic service-station food. 'I'm not sure I'm really... Why are we leaving the motorway?'

His co-conspirator saved him from answering.

'Take the next exit and continue left.'

Nick did as he was told for once and soon they were driving through country lanes.

She was too tired to ask. Nick was going to do what he wanted to do, whether she minded or not, so she might as well save her breath.

After about fifteen minutes they turned down a driveway and he brought the car to a halt. They were parked outside a city-dweller's fantasy cottage: leaded windows, gabled roof, a pretty fence enclosing a half-tamed garden that looked spectacular, even at this time of year.

Nick let out a sharp blast on the horn and Adele winced.

Moments later a man in his thirties came bounding out of the cottage and grinned at Nick as he emerged from the car.

'Nick! Glad you managed to make it after all. Have you got that washing-machine motor you promised me?'

'Sure have. It's in the car, but before I let you have it you have to keep up your end of the bargain—a hearty lunch for two weary travellers.'

The man grinned. 'Phoebe's made one of her famous soups. If you're not careful she'll make you drink a whole vat of it before she lets you continue on your way. Women, huh?'

Adele opened the door and stretched her journey-stiffened legs.

'And talking of women, this must be your missus,' he added. And before Adele could say 'How do you do' he'd ignored the hand she offered and pulled her into a bear hug. She sent Nick a pleading look over the man's shoulder, but all he did was grin back.

'Adele, this is Andy—we've worked on a few projects together.'

Well, that explained the fascination for odd bits of junk and anything mechanical.

Andy finally let her out of his grasp and she gave him a shaky smile.

'Nice to meet you, Adele. I've heard a lot about you. Nick never stops going on about his beautiful, successful wife. I think he's secretly hoping he can give up messing about on film sets and that you'll keep him in the style to which he'd like to become accustomed.'

'Oh.'

Eloquent, Adele. Very impressive. That's a wonderful way to live up to the picture Nick's painted of you.

But Andy didn't seem to notice. He was too busy chatting to Nick as he led them into the cottage. Adele trudged along behind them, forgotten. She let out a large breath and ran her hand through her hair. Thanks to Nick's build-up, Super Adele was going to have to stay for lunch. And, at this precise moment, her alter ego's super powers were glaringly absent.

She watched the two men as she followed them inside and into a cosy lounge complete with inglenook fireplace. Andy dressed like Nick: worn jeans and tops with funky logos or slogans on them. He even had that same mischievous glint in his eye. There had to be a special-effects designers' code or something: *must never grow up and must always be obsessed with green goo and rubber latex body parts.* A whole organisation of Peter Pans. Now, there was a scary thought.

She heard footsteps in the hall and turned to see a woman enter the room. Nick was instantly off his feet and squeezing the life out of her—much the same kind of greeting that Andy had blessed her with.

'Phoebe! It's great to see you again. How's it going?'

Phoebe laughed and smiled as Nick hugged even tighter and rocked her from side to side until she began to lose her balance. A stabbing feeling in her tummy caught Adele by surprise. It didn't ease up, not even when Phoebe whacked Nick on the arm and told him to let her go.

Phoebe wrestled herself away from Nick and turned to face her, still beaming.

'You must be the famous Adele.'

Adele rose from the sofa she was sitting on, her arms and legs suddenly feeling stiff and brittle. She held out a hand. Phoebe raised an eyebrow just a fraction, but shook it anyway.

Words of greeting failed to form an orderly queue in her head. What could she say? These people seemed to know all about her but, until five minutes ago, she'd not even known of their existence. Why? Had she really tuned Nick out every time he'd talked about the fine details of his work? Had she really been that self-absorbed?

'Hello,' she said, trying to smile, but feeling like a cardboard cut-out.

Phoebe smiled back. A proper smile. She'd obviously decided to give her guest the benefit of the doubt. Adele felt as if she'd shrunk an inch or two. If only there were a telephone box somewhere around where she could do a twirl and come out as *her*.

'Come out to the barn, Nick. I want your input on something I'm building. I'm supposed to be making a crazed tennis-ball machine for an ad I'm working on, but it's just refusing to be as diabolical as I want it to be.'

'If you want diabolical, I'm your man,' Nick answered, already starting towards the door.

Phoebe shook her head.

'Lunch will be ready in about twenty minutes, you two. Don't make me come and fetch you, OK?' She turned to Adele and gave her a wink. 'Boys and their toys, right? Our two are worse than most, I suspect. Why don't you come through to the kitchen and we can chat while the men start pulling that machine to bits?'

'Sure.'

She wanted to be bright and sparkling and charming—

Super Adele—but her super powers seemed well and truly buried under a whole heap of other junk. Out of order. Please try again later.

Phoebe seemed really nice. She would go into the kitchen and make small talk and be as pleasant as she knew how to be and ignore the unsettled feeling fluttering in her stomach.

Suddenly, being stuck in the little hatchback with Nick seemed like an attractive prospect. Being here, watching Phoebe potter round the kitchen, was like watching a horror movie. Only this movie had a difference: instead of everything being much, much worse, it was far, far better—what her life should be like, but wasn't.

It was like having her worst failure served up for her so she could choke on every mouthful.

They had it all: the home, the happy marriage. They had roots. Despite herself, she was insanely jealous.

More than anything, Adele wanted roots.

CHAPTER FIVE

WHATEVER Phoebe was stirring in that pot smelled utterly fantastic.

'I hope you like soup. It's broccoli and Stilton.'

'That sounds lovely.' Adele sat down at the breakfast bar and stared blankly at Phoebe's back as she stirred. Then she remembered her resolve to make polite conversation, but it was a bit like when she'd first learned to drive. Nothing came naturally. Every word had to be planned and mentally rehearsed. It took all her concentration.

'How long have you lived here?'

Phoebe tasted the soup and frowned. 'About two years,' she said, adding more salt as she spoke. 'We decided to slow down a little. We both had such hectic work schedules that we hardly saw each other—but I'm sure I don't need to tell you about that.'

Adele dipped her head and fiddled with her fingers. She'd assumed their hosts didn't know about her marital problems. Although she'd been cross Nick hadn't told his family the truth, it wasn't comfortable having her problems out in the open and sullying the atmosphere of perfect domesticity in this cottage.

'My hat goes off to you and Nick if you've found a way to make it work without one of you cutting back on your work.' Phoebe gave a reluctant chuckle. 'I'm sure Andy and I would have been heading for the divorce courts if we hadn't moved here.'

She opened and shut her mouth. Just a lucky guess, then. Her secrets were safe after all.

Phoebe was stirring the soup again. Thank goodness she didn't seem to mind the long gaps in the conversation.

Adele fiddled with a lemon from a bowl on the central island. A move to the country wouldn't have saved her marriage. That would just be a geographical shift. Nick would still be Nick, and Adele would still be Adele, and roses round the door weren't going to suddenly make them compatible.

Phoebe banged the wooden spoon on the saucepan. 'Done. Do you think you can keep an eye on it while I call the lads and get Max?'

Adele nodded. A dog called Max. That was the name she and Nick had picked out for the puppy they were going to get when their respective projects had been put to bed. But then there had been another deal, another project, and the time had never come.

Nick and Andy entered the kitchen a few minutes later, still deep in conversation about mechanics and motors. She shuffled in her seat and waited for Phoebe to return. At least with another female in the room there was a vague possibility the conversation might turn towards something that didn't sound like Klingon.

Phoebe's footsteps outside the kitchen door helped her perk up.

These were nice people. She could chit-chat, if she really put her mind to it. She just needed to get into character, telephone box or no telephone box. She bared her teeth in the beginnings of a smile, but then Phoebe pushed the door open and every molecule in Adele's bloodstream turned to ice.

Max wasn't an Alsatian, or even a Jack Russell. It was much worse than that.

Max was a baby.

A pink, gurgling bundle that sat in his high chair and blew bubbles at Adele while she tried to get her pulse rate under control.

It was official. Babies were now top of her things-to-be-terrified-of list. Worse than spiders by a long shot.

It was OK if she was warned, as she was when she went to Mona's house, but when little dimpled creatures appeared out of the blue she went into a tail-spin. A crawling feeling in her tummy made her want to push back her chair and run.

She couldn't look at him. He was too cute. His intoxicating baby scent was drifting towards her and it was killing her. She sipped warm liquid off her spoon and tried to block it all out.

The chatter around the table filtered away, almost as if she were listening to them talking underwater, and she was left alone with the knowledge that, if things had not gone so disastrously wrong, she would have had a crumpled pink newborn to call her own right this very minute.

She sucked in a breath through her nostrils and tried to shake the images away without actually moving her head. Pictures of her and Nick: laughing in a large cream kitchen, eating soup and taking turns to pace the room with a tiny bundle on their shoulder as it hiccuped.

And then the images became even more disturbing. The confusion she'd felt only days after her husband had walked out on her when she'd found the second pink line on the pregnancy test. The horror a couple of weeks after that when the bleeding had started. And finally, the deep blackness that had shrouded her for months afterwards.

She blinked and her lids stayed closed only a fraction of a second longer than was necessary.

I am not going to cry. I will just harden and harden until I can't feel any more and then I will chat and finish my soup and leave as if nothing was the matter.

It wasn't Andy and Phoebe's fault. She shouldn't punish them by falling to pieces at the lunch table.

It wasn't even Nick's fault. The doctor had said it was one of those things—as though she'd left her umbrella on the bus—and that there was no reason why she shouldn't try again in a couple of months. Only that had been a bit tricky when her husband and his vital ingredients had vanished from her life, never to return.

Adele watched her hosts as, in a strange kind of slow-motion, Andy passed the basket of warm bread to Phoebe and she gave him a little smile.

Such a lot passed between them in that tiny moment and Adele's heart clenched at the memory of times when Nick had looked at her that way. Now he was just glaring at her over his soup.

She'd been wrong. This wasn't a horror story; it was a fairy tale.

And, if she'd believed in fairies and magic, she'd have stepped through the looking glass and taken their places. But this was real life, and real life was cold and hard and ultimately lonely.

There was no way she and Nick were headed for a happy ending.

Nick's eyes never left Adele as he shovelled soup into his mouth. At first everything had seemed fine—the conversation had been flowing, but then he realised it was flowing around her as if she were a rock sat in the middle of a gushing stream. None of it made an impact.

He should have known she'd react like this. It wasn't part of her neatly manicured plan and Adele did not like veering from the plan. Not one little bit.

But, stupidly, he'd hoped that bringing her here might remove the blinkers she wore so firmly strapped to her head. She wasn't even trying. Slow-burning anger warmed his belly.

Phoebe had asked her a question and she hadn't even pre-tended to be interested. She'd just stared into space and ignored her. He'd seen the hurt look on Phoebe's face, caught her eye and shrugged an apology.

How dared Adele do this?

Maybe he should have warned her about his little detour. Maybe he should have warned Andy and Phoebe that things were less than cheery in the Hughes household. But that did not give his darling wife the excuse to behave like a spoilt child. He was going to drag her into this conversation even if she came kicking and screaming. A little civility was not too much to ask.

'What do you think of the soup, Adele?'

She turned to look at him slowly. 'Hmm?'

'The soup. What do you think?'

'Oh.' She hurriedly took another spoonful. 'It's nice.'

Well, monosyllables were better than nothing.

He faced Phoebe and grinned. 'The closest we ever came to home-made soup was buying the over-priced ones in cartons and emptying them into a pan.'

'I've got some recipes for really tasty but easy ones, if you're interested,' Phoebe said, looking hopefully at Adele.

Adele smiled back. Sort of. Progress at last.

'Thank you, but I really don't have time.'

She went back to playing with her soup, although hardly any of it made its way into her mouth.

He'd have done better if he'd let her stay in a sullen lump at one end of the table. Jumping right in and hoping Adele would follow had been a bad idea. That was what he'd tried to do with this whole trip in the first place, and look how that was turning out.

When was he ever going to learn?

The kitchen seemed darker and more oppressive than it had done when they'd started eating and it took Nick a few moments to realise it had nothing to do with Adele's mood and everything to do with the fact it was about to rain. Huge grey clouds hung precariously in the air, darkening the sky as if the sun had just set.

Andy stood up. 'Give us a hand, mate? We left half that motor outside the barn and the bits will rust if they get left out in the rain.'

Nick ran out to join Andy as they scooped various bits of scrap metal off the grass in front of the barn he used as a workshop and dumped them inside. It had always fascinated him how cogs and shafts and odd little shapes fitted together to make something useful. Something that worked—each bit playing its part.

The rain started to splash down in big drops that ran through his hair and down his face as he collected the last pile of stuff.

He'd been so confident when they'd started their journey this morning that he'd be able to win Adele round, but now he wasn't so sure. Their marriage wasn't just on hold, it was lying in pieces and he wasn't sure they could put it all back together and still have something that worked.

Adele swished a damp tea towel round a soup bowl then placed it on the stack with the others. At least she couldn't mess up helping with the dishes. The added bonus was that it was a chore that involved very little talking. None at all, if she were lucky.

She glanced over her shoulder to see Phoebe wiping her son's face and unbuckling the harness of his high-chair. He smiled at her as she lifted him up and immediately thrust his chubby little hand into Phoebe's hair and tugged. She didn't seem to mind. She just laughed and kissed him on the nose.

The dish Adele was wiping slid through the soggy tea towel and didn't even attempt to bounce off the tiled floor.

Nothing could go wrong while wiping up, huh? Famous last words.

'I'm sorry, Phoebe. I should have changed to a fresh towel when this one got damp.'

Phoebe shook her head. 'Don't worry. I drop stuff all the time. I now only ever buy cheap white crockery from the market. It's never hard to find something that matches when the inevitable happens. I'll go and get the broom. Here—' she extended her arms and held Max towards her '—if you could take him, I'll be back in just a tick.'

Adele looked at the little legs swinging in mid-air and swallowed. However, before her mind had made a conscious decision, her hands had found their way under Max's armpits and she drew him to her chest.

Phoebe disappeared out through a little wooden door and Adele was left alone in the kitchen with a warm little body in her arms.

Max had stretched his neck to breaking point almost to follow his mother as she crossed the kitchen and, now that she was gone, he let out a squeal of part-rage, part-despair.

Max didn't understand his mummy was coming back in just a minute and it would do no good to calmly explain that, just because he couldn't see her for a bit, it didn't mean she was gone for ever. Adele stroked his hair and whispered what soothing words she could. The truth that Mummy was coming back soon did nothing to negate this little one's sense of abandonment. She just couldn't communicate that to him. He stiffened against her, arched his back and screamed.

Know how you feel, she thought. Only she'd learned early on that stamping and screaming never worked when the people you loved disappeared. They left anyway and they didn't come back, no matter how good you tried to be.

She tried bouncing Max up and down, hoping his life turned out better. But there was no way Phoebe and Andy would leave this little one to wither away at boarding-school, spending some of the school holidays with distant relations that didn't really have room for him.

Thankfully, Phoebe returned and Max stopped yelling. He seemed quite happy to take hold of her jumper with his fists and babble to himself as long as he could see Phoebe sweeping up the pieces of the broken dish.

He even looked up at her and beamed now he felt safe again. Adele's heart stuttered. He was so adorable, with his tufty black hair and toothless smile. And he smelled so good—of baby powder and innocence. It was all she could do not to cook up a kidnapping plot.

Baby smiles, she decided, were as effective on her armour plating as hydrochloric acid.

Phoebe had just about finished clearing up the mess Adele had made.

'Phoebe? I'm really sorry about the plate. And…and about lunch too. I wasn't a very good guest. I've just got a lot on my mind at the moment. It was nothing personal.'

Phoebe put down the dustpan and brush and turned to lean her bottom against the counter. 'Nick?'

'How did you know?'

'After the looks you were giving each other over the soup, it wouldn't take a genius to work out things aren't peachy in paradise at the moment.'

'Is it that obvious?' Adele's shoulders sagged. 'We're supposed to be fooling the rest of his family we're still madly in love with each other in less than eight hours. The whole thing is going to be a disaster.'

Phoebe tipped her head to one side and looked at the ceiling. 'And let me guess…the idea to wow the in-laws with a united front was…' they both nodded and spoke at the same time '…his.'

'Are you psychic as well as being a fantastic cook?' Adele asked.

Phoebe laughed. 'You seem to forget that Nick and Andy were obviously separated at birth. I've had to put up with similar daft scenarios over the years.'

'Then what's your secret? How have you managed to stay with him without wanting to smother him in his sleep?'

Phoebe gave a rueful smile. 'I have a few techniques I've picked up. Parenting books are a mine of useful information. Turns out that treating him as if he actually was a big kid actually works. I ignore the negative behaviour and praise the good stuff.'

Ignoring the bad stuff? Was that possible? Every time Nick pulled one of his stunts it was like a match to the touch paper. Could she really learn to live with his harem-scarem ways?

'And I've learned to roll with the punches, relax a little. I don't sweat the small stuff any more; I go with the flow.' Phoebe shrugged. 'I've run out of clichés now.'

Adele laughed and Max bounced up and down in her arms and gurgled too, even though he had no idea what was funny. Phoebe walked over and took Max out of Adele's arms.

'Most of all, you have to remember that what they do for a living is create illusions. I don't know about Nick, but Andy is certainly guilty of forgetting that sometimes his version of reality isn't the real deal.'

Adele frowned. She hadn't thought of that. Was that why Super Adele was a constant shadow? What if Nick could see through the illusion to the real Adele underneath?

Funnily enough, that idea filled her with an even greater sense of dread. He'd never known the gawky child that found it hard to make friends and didn't get the grades her parents had expected. She'd worked hard to turn that all around and be who she was now. And that was the woman Nick had loved, maybe even might still love a little bit.

'I'd better go and change this one's nappy.' Phoebe hoisted Max onto her hip and headed for the door.

'Phoebe?'

Phoebe halted, hand on door frame.

Adele smiled. 'Thanks.'

'No problem. Us special effects widows have to stick together.'

Adele sat down at the kitchen table and rested her chin in her hands. Phoebe made it all sound so easy, but it felt like giving in to Nick to treat him like a wayward toddler. She didn't want a big kid to discipline; she wanted a partner. Someone to share the burden, not add to it.

She sighed.

Nick was outside playing with bits of metal, and if she didn't go and get him they would never get to Scotland today. It seemed as if her choice was already made for her.

Nick clenched the steering wheel and tried not to let the words racing round his head burst out on one long, continuous yell.

So much for his brilliant plan.

He'd visualised the visit as the perfect opportunity to show Adele how happy Andy and Phoebe were, and how they had managed to make their different lifestyles mesh together.

Come on! If their home were any more perfect, little cartoon bluebirds would be coming to rest on Phoebe's fingers when she hung the washing out!

But Adele couldn't see any of that. She was stuck in her it-can-never-work rut and would not be pulled out of it. The scary thing was, he suspected he was teetering on the edge and was just about to slide down into the ditch to join her.

Where was the funny, sexy woman he'd married? Sure, she'd always been a little high-maintenance, but that was half the fun. When they'd first got together, he could have honestly put his hand on his heart and sworn she was the perfect woman. And even after their big fight, he had still believed it. It was only when she'd shut him out of her life completely that he'd started to suspect she might be slightly tarnished.

And part of him was angry with her for that—for not living up to the promise on the outside of the box.

The swirling words got too much for him and he realised he had to let some of them out before he imploded.

'What the heck was wrong with you back there, Adele?'

See? She'd always said she wanted the direct approach and now he was giving it to her. She ought to be proud of him.

Adele didn't move her forehead off the passenger window, but answered in a weary voice. 'I'm not talking to you when you're being like this.'

'Like what? Rude? Like you were at Andy and Phoebe's?'

She closed her eyes. 'I didn't mean to be rude. Just drop it, Nick.'

'No, I won't drop it. You embarrassed me in front of my friends. If you ever do something like that again, so help me I'll—'

'What? Divorce me? It's too late for that threat, remember?'

He pressed his teeth together until the muscles at the sides of his jaw started to twitch. He turned the windscreen wipers up a notch to deal with the rain pounding on the car.

The metallic voice of the satellite-navigation system pierced the atmosphere.

'In thirteen hundred feet, continue right.'

Adele snorted. 'Continue right? What does that mean?'

He tried to keep his voice even. 'It means the left-hand lane is about to feed into the slip-road and we need to keep right if we want to stay on the motorway.'

'Can't we turn the stupid thing off?'

Nick took his eyes off the road momentarily and looked across at Adele in the passenger seat.

'What is it about the satellite-navigation system that really bothers you?'

She stiffened. 'It doesn't bother me. It's just unnecessary. We're on a motorway going north for the next hundred miles at least. All it does is tell us the obvious.'

'You hate it.'

She fidgeted in her seat.

'I… Oh…'

'And shall I tell you why you hate it?'

Adele turned to look at him. He was about to turn psychologist on her? This she had got to hear!

'Fire away, professor.'

'You don't like handing the control over to somebody else, even if it's just a bit of machinery that could make your life easier.'

'That is *so* not true. I use machines at work all the time.'

'Not the point. You're so flipping independent, Adele. I'm surprised you actually let your computer crunch numbers for you instead of getting your abacus out and doing it yourself.'

'Well, that was a very grown-up response. I'm glad you took the time to share that.'

'Don't do that.'

'I'm not doing anything other than trying to be the adult in this scenario.'

'Well, it's a pity you didn't think of that back at Andy and Phoebe's house, isn't it? You acted like a spoiled brat, so don't come all high and mighty and *I'm being the grown-up* on me!'

Adele folded her arms and glared at what she could see of the carriageway through the driving rain.

She didn't have an answer to that.

And the reason she didn't have an answer was that Nick was spot-on.

Her voice was soft when she answered a minute later. 'I apologised to Phoebe while you were out in the shed.'

He shot her an incredulous look, but didn't accuse her further.

'Well, I'm glad you came to your senses. They're a great couple.'

'I know.'

He flicked the indicator and overtook a caravan.

'Why do you insist on cutting yourself off from people, Adele?'

'I…'

She frowned. Did she?

'Do I?' she asked.

Nick shook his head. 'You certainly shut *me* out.'

'Don't be silly.'

'You talk to Mona, but you won't talk to me. Why am I always kept at arm's length?'

She didn't know. It was just easier to be herself with Mona. She was a good friend, but her world wouldn't crumble if they fell out. So much more was at stake with Nick. She didn't want to let him down.

She looked at him. She'd already disappointed him today. There wasn't much point in digging herself in deeper by making more excuses.

Nick shook his head then indicated at a sign on the grass verge. 'Service station. I need a break.'

CHAPTER SIX

THERE was a sharpness in the air Adele hadn't expected when she stepped out of the car. The Lake District wasn't far away. They were two hundred and fifty miles north of London and it was noticeably colder. Snow dusted the fells to the north. She reached inside her pockets for her gloves.

Nick seemed happy to hurry into the low building of the service station, but she took her time as she walked across the car park.

She loved this kind of landscape. It was proud, ancient and soul-achingly lonely. Rolling green hills covered in scrubby grass dipped down into a valley where a rocky little stream gurgled along. Sheep dotted the banks, meandering in and out of neighbouring fields through the crumbling dry-stone walls.

Clean, cold air filled her lungs as she took one deep breath. Just being here was detoxifying. She turned one full circle before entering the services, just to take it all in.

The building was obviously not owned by one of the large chains—there were no fast-food counters or slot machines and as she entered the restaurant she was relieved to see wooden tables and chairs, real plants and exposed timber beams supporting the roof.

Nick was standing at the counter waiting to order coffee and she stood silently next to him. When his order came he handed her a large latte and the fattest, moistest slice of chocolate cake she'd ever seen. Then he walked off to a table and sat down without saying a word.

She slid into the chair opposite him.

'Talk to me, Nick.'

He stirred his coffee. She'd never seen him like this before. Where were the smart retorts? The jokes? Suddenly she missed them. Usually he had the irritating ability to just snap out of being angry, as if he'd flicked a switch or something.

'I'm sorry I let you down, truly I am.' Nick dropped his spoon in surprise. She knew it wasn't often that word passed her lips. 'I was out of my depth and you kind of sprang the visit on me, after all.'

'I didn't think visiting friends would be such a big deal. I thought we'd have a nice time.'

'Your friends, though. I didn't feel comfortable at all. What on earth had you told them about me? What was all that "famous Adele" business?'

He snorted. 'Great! Now I'm in trouble for saying nice things about my wife?'

She pressed her lips together and pondered her answer. How could she tell him it was very hard to admit she was going under? All she heard was: *You're so wonderful, Adele*, or *You can do anything, Adele*. He always seemed to expect her to cope with everything he flung at her, and so she did.

'No, that's not it at all. I used to love the fact you believed in me so much, but you don't understand the pressure it puts me under. You're just like my parents in that respect. I didn't want to disappoint you.'

He put his coffee-cup down and stared at her. 'Well, you did.'

'See? As soon as I admit I'm not the oh-so-perfect picture you paint of me, I've let you down. Sometimes I just want to be Adele, without the adjectives. Not "successful" or "famous" or "fabulous". Just me.'

'But you *are* all of those things.'

The look he gave her made tears prickle behind her eyes. She knew he thought that and, while it melted her heart that he held her in such high regard, on the other hand she wanted him to see right through the illusion.

'I'm not who you think I am.'

He took a sip of his coffee and studied her. She refused to flinch under his gaze.

'I'm starting to see that.'

Suddenly she wanted to take it all back, to stop him seeing what a fraud she was. It felt too raw to have him peeling away the layers one by one.

They sat in silence while Adele took comfort in her chocolate cake and they finished their coffees. As she started to pile the crockery up on the tray, he spoke.

'Maybe I've been guilty of asking the impossible of you, believing in you too much, if you like, but you do the opposite. You don't believe in me enough.'

She stopped stacking, opened her mouth to speak then paused as a cup slid off the pile. She carefully replaced it, only letting go when she was sure it was perfectly balanced.

She spoke without taking her eyes off it. 'Is this about the job? Because you know—'

'It all comes back to the flipping job in America, doesn't it? Are you ever going to be able to forgive me for that?'

She didn't answer.

'We could have worked something out, you know. It would have been difficult for a few months, but it wasn't the end of the world. You could have come with me, even just for short visits.'

'But my job, the house—' Her roots.

'Are the most important things in your life. I know that now.'

'I couldn't just drop everything at a moment's notice. You didn't even give me time to work out a plan. It was now or never. And you chose now for the job and never for me. How do you think I felt when I realised you hadn't just gone down the pub to cool off, when I got your text message saying you'd call me when you landed in LA?'

He shrugged and crossed his arms over his chest, leaning back in his seat. 'You were the one who told me to get on the plane.'

'I was angry, Nick! I didn't think you'd actually do it! Stop being so pigheaded.'

'Then why, if you wanted to sort it out later, did you not answer any of my calls? It gave a pretty clear message, you know.'

She swallowed. She couldn't tell him here. Not like this. The backs of her eyes stung. How could she tell him that at first she'd been too thrown by what should have been the happiest news of her life to know what to do? Then, just as she'd been gearing herself up to ring him and say 'Guess what? You're going to be a dad!' it suddenly wasn't true any more.

She hadn't been able to tell him. She hadn't been able to tell anyone. Only Mona. And Mona only knew because she had been there when it had started, had held her hand at the hospital. Then she'd taken her home and hugged her until the tears had run dry.

Those were things *he* should have done! He should have been there. And she'd been so angry at him for being thousands of miles away she hadn't been able to talk to him.

Her lip did a micro-quiver, but she bit down on it before it developed into the real thing.

The one time she'd really needed him, he hadn't been there for her. And it didn't matter that the sensible side of her brain understood that he hadn't known, that he'd have been there if he could have been. The messy, illogical side of her couldn't quite forgive him. Somehow it had summed up all that was wrong with their marriage—Nick happily bounding along, oblivious to her feelings.

Even now the anger was raging inside her.

'It doesn't matter now, Nick. It's water under the bridge. We both know it would have ended sooner or later. We just don't work as a team.'

His voice was emotionless. 'So you say.' He let his gaze wander round the room and she saw him stare as something caught his interest.

She twisted her head to catch a look. Over in the far corner a woman sat with a baby, trying to comfort it as she waited for its milk to warm in a jug of hot water. Adele turned back to look at him. He looked downtrodden.

He shrugged it off. 'Just as well all that "trying for a baby" stuff was a disaster. What a mess that would have been.'

She nodded. The words were caught up in the back of her throat with her next breath.

She wanted him to make a joke of it as he had done all those months ago. Every time the pregnancy test had been quietly negative he'd given her a hug and said, 'Never mind, we're having fun practising.' She'd loved him for making her smile, even though she'd known he was bitterly disappointed too.

She needed him to do that now, to make the sick feeling go away.

But he looked blank, as if all the cheeky humour had leached out of him. And even worse was the knowledge that she had been the cause. She'd eventually brought him down to earth and it was killing him.

Nick picked up the tray. 'Are you finished?'

Yes, she was finished. The whole thing was finished.

The sun was low in the sky as they got back on the motorway, giving a warm glow to clouds that otherwise had an ominous hint of steel. Nick stared out of the passenger window. Adele was back in the driving seat—in more ways than one.

'How are we going to handle the party, Nick?'

What was to handle?

'How do you mean? We walk in, we smile, we talk, we eat, we leave.'

Adele sighed. 'As always, you haven't thought this through, have you?'

He hunched down in his seat a little further. 'Obviously not.'

'There's no need to be sarcastic.'

Maybe there wasn't, but it made him feel better. Adele had sat as judge and jury on their relationship and she wasn't about to share the power and let him have a second chance. He understood that now.

'OK, OK. What have I missed?'

'Look at us! We've both got faces like a wet weekend. No one's going to believe we're love's young dream. Phoebe sussed us out in an instant.'

His eyebrows inched up. 'She did?'

'Women spot these things. Your sisters will be on to us in the blink of an eyelid.'

'We'll have to smile an awful lot more and convince them.'

Adele went quiet and they sat with the sound of the engine for company for a while. Big fat splashes started appearing on the windscreen and he realised that it wasn't rain this time, it was snow—big, fluffy flakes of the Christmas-card variety.

Adele turned the wipers on and the action seemed to kick-start her brain again too.

'It feels too much like lying to them, Nick. I don't like it.'

'All we've got to do is be civil to each other, talk, smile a bit. We can still do that, can't we? We don't have to be all over each other on the dance floor or anything.'

She didn't sound convinced. 'I suppose so.'

'We can split up and circulate. All my family will be there and they'll want to hear about my job in LA. Hell, they'll be wrestling me to the ground and demanding free tickets to the première if I know them!'

Miracle of miracles, Adele cracked a smile.

'OK. That sounds like a plan. We arrive together and we circulate as much as possible, meeting up every now and then for a progress report. Your sisters will all be keen to fill me in on the latest news about our myriad nephews and nieces— that should take up a fair chunk of time.' She nodded to herself as she stared at the carriageway. 'Yes. It might work. But only if we keep our distance from each other.'

It was crazy enough to work: stay apart to convince everyone they were together.

If only Adele didn't seem so overjoyed at the prospect of avoiding him for the whole of the evening.

As they drove further north, the snow eased off. They'd obviously driven under the snow cloud and out the other side. They reached the fringes of the Lake District and the temperature dropped further. A thin coating of snow carpeted the valleys and clung in drifts to the craggy peaks.

But this wasn't fresh snow. There must have been a fall last night. He had no idea if more was supposed to be on the way. He did, however, know a woman who would.

'Adele? What's the weather forecast for this area today?'

She hesitated—he guessed she was considering feigning ignorance; she hated being thought predictable—but instead she gave in and spoke in a weary voice.

'Rain with the possibility of icy showers, clearing towards evening. That's what the man on the radio said, anyway. We should have seen the worst of it by now.'

'Good. The roads are clear enough at the moment, but I wouldn't like it to get any worse. That would really slow us down.' He checked his watch. 'It's just before four. We're a little behind schedule, but we should still be there with an hour or more to spare.'

Adele's smile was wry. 'Be careful, Nick. You're starting to sound organised.'

'What I really meant to say was: shouldn't we be going south if we're heading for Scotland?'

'That's more like the Nick Hughes I know.'

She missed out the *and love*. He smiled anyway. 'I don't like to disappoint a lady.'

Nick laid his head back on the headrest and closed his eyes. What he'd said was spot-on. She wasn't the only one disappointing her spouse. He might have just brushed over the truth of it with a joke, but just once he would like her to look at him the way she had in the early days of their marriage. She'd thought he was wonderful then. He hadn't changed; he was still the same old Nick, but nowadays everything he said and did seemed to be wrong.

'Oh, bother!'

He opened his eyes to find out what had caused Adele's outburst. A string of red brake lights snaked up the hill in front of them. Very soon they joined the back of the queue. The traffic was moving at ten miles an hour at best.

Nick stared angrily at the bumper of the car in front. 'Well, that's just great! If we don't get moving again quickly, we're going to miss dinner.'

The line of cars was at least a mile long, and possibly longer, as the road curved up and round a hill, blocking his vision.

'Do you think it's the snow?' Adele asked as she spritzed the windscreen with screen wash for the fiftieth time. 'We all know it only takes three flakes of the stuff to bring the great British transport system to a halt.'

'Shouldn't be. The gritters have been out and the carriage-way is clear. It's probably an accident—some fool going too fast in these conditions.'

'I hope it isn't serious,' she said in a small voice.

'Me too.'

Five minutes later they were hardly moving at all.

'My calf muscle is aching from keeping my foot on the clutch,' Adele moaned. 'I'd prefer to be at a complete stop than this interminable crawling along. I don't want to get stuck in this. Do you remember that story on the news a few years ago? It snowed and hundreds of people got stuck on the motorway in East Anglia and had to spend the night in their cars.'

'That's not going to happen here.'

'How do you know? We're only doing…' she peered at the speedometer '…two miles an hour. Any slower and we'd be going backwards.'

Nick frowned but didn't say anything. Adele craned her neck to look out of the back window. 'There's at least a hundred cars behind us as well. It's not like we've got much choice.'

An idea started to sharpen out of the fog at the back of his brain. 'Maybe not.'

She shot him a look of desperation. 'Please, don't tell me you've been taking stunt-driving lessons, as you've always threatened you would, and you want to drive over the top of all the other cars until we're clear.'

'Tempting—but no.'

Adele punched him on the right arm.

'I've been climbing in this area a few times, remember? I think we're not far from Kendal. If I'm right, there should be a junction in a mile or so. We can take the road into the town then get on the A6. After about ten miles, it runs almost parallel to the motorway. We could leapfrog over the jam and join the motorway again at the next junction.'

'That sounds frighteningly like a good plan.'

He did a little bow—well, as much as his seat belt would allow him.

Adele flicked the sat nav with her finger. 'See? It's saying nothing. Your little gizmo couldn't come up with an idea like that.'

'Nope. She's a lot like you.'

'Don't call it *she*. And do not start comparing me with that thing. I hate it.'

He laughed. 'Well, I see a certain similarity. She's programmed to get to Invergarrig by the quickest route and she's going to stick doggedly to the plan, no matter what. She won't be of any use to us if we wing it.'

'Are you saying I'm a machine? That I can't…' she paused, as if it was difficult for her to even say the words '…*wing* it?'

'Calm down. I'm just saying I don't need *two* bossy women in my life at the moment.'

As Adele breathed in, the atmosphere in the car thickened.

'Well, I've told you I'm seeing my solicitor as soon as we get back. I can't clear off any quicker than that! If you didn't want me around, you shouldn't have asked me to come with you.'

He leaned forward and pressed a button on the side of the satellite-navigation unit. His voice was gentle when he spoke. 'No, you daft woman. I didn't mean you; I meant *her*. She's got a fixed idea of where she's going and how she's going to get there and she's just going to make a fuss if we deviate. It's time to turn it off and follow our instincts.'

'Oh.'

Nick risked a look at her when she was concentrating on the road ahead. Her shoulders had dropped an inch and the faint remnant of a self-satisfied smirk lingered round her lips.

'You, I can deal with,' he said, reaching across and rubbing her forearm as it rested on the gear stick. 'Her—going *bing, bing, bing* and *please do a U-turn*—not so much.'

They smiled at each other and it was as if all the tension had melted away. For once they were united against a common enemy, even if it was an electrical harridan.

Perhaps there was hope. Perhaps it could be him and Adele against the world again, instead of the pair of them clawing away at each other. And, for a moment, Adele seemed to echo his thoughts.

She smiled a sweet smile at him and his stomach did a triple flip. Then she opened her mouth and the flimsy hopes he'd balanced one upon another tumbled.

'See, Nick? As friends we work. Now we've made a decision about our future we don't have to push and pull any more. If we can keep this up for the rest of the weekend we'll be home and dry. It'll be better for your family too. Once they know the truth, they'll see we can maintain a civil relationship and the news of our separation will be easier for them.'

The voice in his head had a hard edge of sarcasm. *How thoughtful of you.*

There she went again. Making sure everyone else was OK—especially Adele. God forbid anyone should ever think she was less than perfect. All this treacly stuff about being better for his family was tosh. Adele just didn't want to be the bad guy in this scenario and she was pleased as punch she could walk out on their marriage without a pang of guilt.

And all the time she was bolstering her own defences, she was twisting the knife one more time into his unguarded flesh.

She just carried on chattering as if she'd had the greatest revelation ever.

'We were good friends once, before we started going out, weren't we?'

He nodded.

'Well, we can have that again, can't we?'

Why did she have to end every sentence in a question that required a yes or no answer from him? He didn't want to be pushed into agreeing with her. Couldn't she just leave him be?

He answered because he had to. 'It worked once.'

'Exactly. Just friends.'

He sneered. Just as well she was changing gear so they could edge forward once again and she didn't see it. 'Friends it is.'

Only he'd never wanted to be *just friends* with Adele. That had been her idea. From the moment they'd been introduced at a dinner party held by a mutual friend he'd known she was different. Special. He'd been captivated by her quick mind, her drive, the prim exterior with just a hint of something else simmering underneath.

He'd agreed to exactly the same thing the first time she'd turned him down.

Friends it is.

He'd been lying then and he was lying now.

It had taken time to crack her tough outer shell and get her to agree to a proper date. When he'd kissed her at the end of the evening all his fantasies about her had been proved right. Adele was a passionate and deeply sexy woman. She just liked to hide it well.

Soon he'd realised he hadn't beaten down the last of her defences. Under that exterior was another shell and another. And, in the centre, one so hard he now thought it might never crack.

She had never truly shared herself with him. There was always an elusive piece of herself she held back. It didn't matter he knew that it stemmed from her childhood when her mother had left her behind, aged eight, so she could travel the world with her high-flying father.

Eight. It was an awfully young age to harden oneself into a tough little ball.

Adele had dealt with it the only way she knew how. She drove herself to be successful in business to get her father's attention. Little else worked—he'd seen that for himself. And she'd become fiercely independent, never letting anyone close enough to damage her in the same way again.

He knew all of that. And it didn't help one bit.

Until now he'd foolishly thought, with enough time, he'd be able to soften the hard place inside her and see her unfurl. But now he had to admit it might never happen. The odds were a million to one and he was starting to question his own dogged loyalty.

He wanted a soul mate, a partner. And, as much as he loved Adele, he was starting to question if she was capable of that kind of intimacy.

'Finally!' Adele yelled, snapping him back to reality. 'I can see the slip-road. Another minute or two and we'll be on our way. You'll have to give me directions. I've never been here before, so without you I'm totally lost.'

'Sure.' If only she could hear herself.

He'd wanted Adele to trust him with the rest of her life and she'd whittled it down to just one hour.

'This doesn't look good.'

Adele leaned forward and tried to peer at the clouds overhead. Nick had suggested they swap places once they'd got off the motorway, arguing it would be easier for him to navigate as he drove rather than barking instructions at her.

She had been overjoyed at the thought of giving her left leg a rest.

Besides, the scenery round here was stunning. She was quite happy drinking in the views of the ancient mountains and deep valleys that made this area such a tourist hot spot in the summer months. Draped in white, it just looked magical. Off the main road, the snow was much deeper, with drifts reaching a couple of feet up against the farm gates and hedgerows.

But it was as she was staring upwards at the ragged hilltops that she noticed the iron-grey clouds. And then the flakes that started whirling high in the sky and slowly spiralling down.

'Do you think we ought to turn back and go into Kendal?' she asked. 'We only passed through about fifteen minutes ago.'

Nick shook his head. 'It's not falling too fast at the moment and, with any luck, we'll be back on the motorway before it gets too bad.'

She pulled her gloves on a little tighter. Somehow the action made her feel more protected. And it certainly did help to make sure her fingers were as warm as they could be. The overstretched heater in her little car was only just bringing the temperature up to a bearable level.

The wipers speeded up another notch as Nick flicked the switch. Snow was hurling itself at the glass now and they were struggling to bat it aside.

'Are you sure you know where you're going?'

'Adele! Can you not just trust me for once? I've been here at least three times before.'

'So you recognise where we are now, do you?'

'Yes,' he answered without hesitation, then stopped to take in the surrounding area. 'Well, no…not exactly, now you mention it. The snow makes it all very different. But we're on the right road and if we don't get in a panic, everything will be fine.'

'No one's panicking.'

'I don't even have to look at you to know that every muscle in your body is starting to clench.'

'Rubbish!'

Still, she circled her ankle slightly, trying to ease the cramp that was threatening to engulf her left calf. But that was nothing to do with Nick. She was just stiff from the traffic jam.

Nick shot a look across at her and the movement of her foot caught his attention.

'Oh, for goodness' sake! Look, I'll turn the blasted sat nav on if you're that worried. All she wants to do is get us back on the motorway and she won't take no for an answer.' He leaned forward and pressed the button. 'Happy?'

The stupid thing binged into life, all chirpy and self-satisfied.

'Continue straight for three-point-seven miles.'

Nick gave a smug smile and raised his eyebrows, as if to say, *See? We were going the right way after all.*

She folded her arms across her chest. 'Do what you like. I didn't ask you to put it on.'

'But you're happier now it is, aren't you?'

'No.'

She didn't want to be, which was almost the same thing, wasn't it? She stretched her legs and discovered the cramp in her calf had mysteriously vanished.

CHAPTER SEVEN

'*IN FIVE hundred feet, turn right.*'

Nick made a noise of surprise and gave the satellite navigation system a hefty flick with his index finger.

'Leave it alone, Nick. Its goal in life is to get us back on the motorway. You said so yourself.'

He gave her an incredulous look. Her only response was a little shrug, as if to say *what*?

Nick shook his head. He should've guessed the women would gang up on him.

'It's probably a more direct route. You did say you've only been here three times before, didn't you?'

'Yes…'

'So what's the problem? Do as you're told for once.'

Nick said nothing and indicated right. He was lucky he didn't snap the flimsy plastic lever right off.

'With any luck we'll get back on the motorway a little quicker,' she said, looking out of the window. 'This snow is easing off, but I'll still be glad when we're off the back roads.'

He slowed to take the corner. The road seemed even quieter than the one they had been travelling on, but the satellites could obviously see through the clouds and snow and knew where they were heading.

Ten minutes later and it seemed they'd gone so far past the

back of beyond they surely were about to drop off the edge of the world. Even the ever-present sheep were absent. He scoured the landscape for any clue they were nearing the motorway and, hopefully, civilisation again.

'Are you sure this is the right way, Nick?'

Nick felt himself bristle. Why did she always have to question him? Why could she not just trust him on one small thing? It didn't help that he knew she was like this with everyone. He wanted her to be different with him, to relax her rigid need for control and have faith in him for once.

'To be honest, no. But I'm sitting here like a good boy with my hands on the steering wheel and doing as I'm told, all right?'

'Fine. Not saying a word. Drive on.'

She shivered and rubbed herself with her gloved hands. The heater was not having much of an impact against the freezing temperatures.

They drove in silence but he refused to let himself feel uneasy. What had been a good-sized single carriageway had narrowed so a couple of cars could pass each other, but if a tractor or a van appeared it would be a squeeze. Then it became a single track with passing places and the lack of traffic meant the snow was deeper than just a dusting. At least the last few flakes of snow had dwindled and it wasn't getting any worse.

He kept his eyes on the road, even as he sensed Adele looking across at him. *Doing as I'm told, for once.* He tried to radiate it through every pore. Thankfully, she decided not to go there and pressed her mouth closed again.

He knew her resolve was pushed to breaking point as the snow thickened and they rumbled along the track. The car bumped to a halt as the road seemed almost to vanish and they were left staring at an opening in the dry-stone wall where a gate was wedged open and the track continued.

She looked at him, eyebrows raised. He wasn't having any

of it. She'd issued him a challenge and he was going to prove to her she could trust him, if only in this one small thing. She'd always moaned he couldn't stick to anything.

He tapped the screen of the sat nav, drawing her attention to the red line showing their route was still straight ahead, then crunched the car into gear, still holding her gaze. He only took his eyes away when he needed to negotiate the narrow gap in the wall.

At first, it was fine. They drove across a flat expanse of field, but before long the ridges in the ground marking the track blurred into the snow and there was no telling exactly where they should be heading. He slowed to a stop.

He closed his eyes and waited for the sigh he knew was coming. Adele always let out a great shuddering breath before she started with the recriminations. In fact, sometimes the sigh was enough on its own. In the months before they'd separated he'd heard it plenty of times.

Maybe he should have realised that, in some small way, she'd given up on him when she'd stopped voicing her frustrations. Stupidly, he'd thought some of the things that always bothered her had stopped being such an issue, thought that perhaps finally she got it.

Couldn't she have understood that he'd been working himself so hard so that they'd have a better future together? And for a while it had looked as if it were going to pay off. Now he'd worked on one of Tim's films he could pick and choose his projects. He'd be able to spend more time at home, less time disappearing at a moment's notice. When the baby arrived, they would have been able to slow down a bit.

But, true to form, things had not gone according to plan. How, when teenage girls seemed to fall pregnant at the drop of a hat, had it taken more than ten months for him and Adele to get nowhere? It seemed the more you wanted a baby, the harder it was to actually create one.

And now there was no guarantee there would ever be a baby. And, if she had her way, there wouldn't be an Adele either—at least not for him.

'Nick?'

There was a soft quality to her voice that jerked him back to the present.

'I think I can see a light up ahead. It might be another car. That could be the main road.'

The snowy landscape was now a pale lavender. The sun was almost ready to set behind the hills and, if they didn't get a move-on, they'd be stuck with very little hint of a road in the pitch blackness. Still, he held off stepping on the accelerator.

Adele punched him on the arm and pointed. 'There it is again!'

Sure enough, he saw a flicker of a light up ahead and off to the right. It might be a car; it might not. Even if it were a house, at least they could ask directions. The light wavered and disappeared for a second or so, then reappeared a little way away. Whatever it was, it was moving—and that was good news. Forward seemed the only sensible choice at the moment.

He put the car into gear and started off slowly and, as they neared the brow of the hill, he noticed an open gate on the other side of the field and steered straight towards it. Adele's little car squeezed easily between the gateposts and he relaxed a little once through them.

The road was better defined here, but it was getting darker by the second. He switched the headlights onto half-beam and checked the sat nav by tapping the corner of the display so it repeated its last set of instructions.

'In one thousand feet, continue to the left.'

Adele sat up straighter next to him. 'What does that mean? Continue forward or turn left?'

He shrugged. 'Probably just a fork in the road—probably a farm track—and it's telling us our road is the one to the left.'

'Oh.' She relaxed back into her seat and rubbed her hands together.

'Of course, it could also mean a sharp bend in the road. Sometimes it gets confused.'

'I thought it was infallible.'

'No, my darling wife. That would be you.'

He saw Adele's hands fly up into the air out of the corner of his eye. 'I can't believe you won't let that old argument lie. I'm as capable as the next person of admitting I'm wrong.'

Nick snorted. Adele's memory was occasionally rather selective. How about the time she'd ranted and raved at the online supermarket when the shopping hadn't turned up? They'd apologised and pointed out that she'd entered the wrong postcode, which had confused their system. But oh, no, that can't have been it. Adele was adamant she knew her own postcode and that it had to be a glitch with their computers. Never mind the fact he'd caught her making the same mistake a few weeks later when filling out a form.

But that was small stuff he'd tried hard not to sweat about and he wasn't going to start it now. And if it had all been minor mistakes like that, perhaps it wouldn't have irritated him so much, but he guessed that if Adele couldn't admit to forgetting her postcode, she certainly wasn't going to own up to sabotaging her own marriage.

No, no. Perfect Adele would never do such a thing.

He was angry with her—for always putting up a glossy front and never letting him see the real woman underneath—and also angry with himself. Now he could see the sometimes-scared, sometimes-vulnerable Adele she tried so hard to hide, he had a worrying urge to protect her. And all he would get if he tried to do just that would be a kick in the face, and that made him cross all over again.

So he concentrated on the snowy road and alternated between frustration and compassion. Finally he could stand the whirling thoughts no longer. He had to break the cycle somehow.

'So, you're not infallible, huh? Does that mean you are going to admit you had a part in ending our marriage, or is that all down to yours truly?'

He was ashamed at the bitter edge to his words. He'd never talked to her like this before, but no matter how he'd tried to soften his tone, it came out harsh and belligerent.

She said nothing for a few seconds. He couldn't look across and check her expression as he couldn't risk taking his eyes off the snow-covered track, even for a split-second. The snow was darkening to a bluish-grey in the failing light and there was less contrast between it and the rough grass that poked through and marked the edges of the track.

She sighed, long and hard.

'OK, I admit it. I still think you dumped a major decision on me too suddenly, but I didn't help matters by digging my heels in…'

He waited, partly because he could tell she had more to say and partly because he was too shocked to form any words of his own.

'And I should have returned your calls after you left,' she added. 'Or, at the very least, I should have answered them. I just…'

This time he wasn't so patient. 'Just…what?'

Her voice was so quiet he had to strain to hear it above the hum of the engine. 'I just…couldn't.'

That was the best explanation she could give? Unbelievable. He knew that he should be triumphant with her admission that she wasn't the only one to have made bad choices, but suddenly it wasn't enough.

Soft flakes started to fall on the windscreen again and he

smiled darkly to himself. He'd always said it would be a cold day in hell before Adele acknowledged she was wrong about anything and the weather seemed oddly fitting.

He needed more. He needed to know why she had found it so easy to let go of their marriage—of him—when she held on to everything else in her life with an iron grip.

'Why couldn't you, Adele? What stopped you?'

He knew the answer. Pride. But he wanted to hear her say it. Just this once.

He heard her intake of breath as she opened her mouth to answer, but she was cut off by a metallic voice barking instructions:

'Continue left.'

He was very tempted to echo Adele's earlier outburst at the blasted thing and tell it to shut up, but every ounce of his attention was suddenly required in making sense of the scene in front of him.

There was no fork in the road, no farm track to avoid. There wasn't even a road in front of him. Just swirling flakes lit up by the headlights against a grey background of air and space.

He yanked the wheel hard to the left and squeezed the brake pedal until it reached the floor. The car turned but the back end carried on skidding to the side. Adele let out a short, sharp scream and braced herself against the dashboard.

Somehow, he remembered to turn the wheels into the skid and the car came slowly to a halt. He needed to get his bearings, find out how things had gone so drastically wrong, so he opened the door and jumped out of the car, and almost instantly backed up so he was pressed against the closed rear door.

He didn't care about the icy specks that dampened his hair and face. All he could see was the small cliff only a couple of feet in front of him. All he could imagine was a battered car at the bottom.

'Nick?' Adele's voice was faint. He heard it, but somehow couldn't register it.

He blinked and looked down the short cliff again. It was only a drop of ten feet or so, but enough to do damage to both the car and its occupants. A sheep bleated and stared back at him, clearly wondering how anyone could be so stupid.

He was asking himself the very same question.

He got slowly into the car again and pressed himself back into his seat by pushing away with straightened arms on the steering wheel. If only he'd kept his emotions in check, brushed it all off as he normally did, then he wouldn't have lost concentration.

A cold feeling tingled inside him. Fear. It wasn't just a mangled car he'd imagined at the bottom of the cliff, but also a twisted and broken Adele. And it would have been all his fault.

All his petty niggles about who was right and who was wrong now seemed hollow. None of that mattered. All he could think about, all he could taste in his mouth, was horror at the prospect of losing her.

'Nick? Are you all right?' Her voice seemed to drift in from far away.

He opened his eyes slowly and turned to look at her. 'That was close.'

Her eyes were wide, her face pale. 'I know, but we're OK. Let's just get out of here and get back onto the main road— any main road. I don't care what that thing of yours says, I just want to see white lines and two-way traffic again.'

Without that thing of his they would have…

He started the car up again and took a good look at the road before he pulled away. The track had turned sharply to the left—almost a right angle—and now dipped down a steep hill. He went slowly, but even so, the wheels slid on the ice hidden under the fresh dusting of snow. He kept control—just—and brought them to a stop at the bottom of the hill.

There was another gate, but this one was closed. Adele nodded, sharing his thoughts, it seemed, and got out of the car. After a minute or so he joined her.

'It's no good, Nick. There's a chain through the latch and it's padlocked. We can't get through.'

Nick rattled the chain. It was rusty but surprisingly solid. The padlock was new and shiny. No hope of shifting it at all. He swore and marched back to the car, grabbed the sat nav from its cradle and zoomed out to get a bigger map of the area. The stupid thing was right. If they could keep going for another mile or two, they'd be back on a main road and much closer to the motorway than when they'd started off.

Good intentions, but a little lacking on essential information. A bit like him really.

One gate. One obstacle was all it had taken to bring them to a grinding halt. The only thing for it was to retrace their steps and see if they could get back to where they'd been earlier.

He watched Adele climb into the car again and clap the powdery snow off her gloves. If only relationships were that easy too. What he wouldn't give to retrace his steps, take a ride back in time, and return to before the point when the cracks started appearing in their life together. But it didn't work that way. Time marched on and you always ended up further along the path you'd chosen, no matter which direction you travelled.

She looked at him, her face strangely expressionless. 'What now?'

'Only one thing for it. We turn round and go back the way we came, then on to Invergarrig. We'll be late for the meal, but we should still get there before midnight.'

'Do you want me to phone your mum and let her know we're going to be late?'

He smiled, but it was half-hearted. 'That would be great.'

At least Adele's organised nature meant she always thought of little details like that, he thought. Mum would worry if they weren't there on time and he didn't want to give her any more stress.

He did a three-point turn while Adele reached for her phone, took her gloves off, punched a couple of buttons then held it to her ear. A few seconds later she pulled it away to stare at the display.

'No signal.'

Nick looked up the hill in front of him. 'Must be because we're down in a dip. Mobile-phone coverage is a little patchy in this area at the best of times. Try again when we get to the top of the hill.'

She nodded and folded her hands in her lap, phone clasped between them.

He revved the engine and started to move the little car up the hill. The first third was fine as the incline was a little shallower there, but as soon as they tried to go any further, the wheels just spun and the car started to slide backwards.

Changing gear didn't help much. They only moved another fifteen feet before gravity and ice conspired to send them back to the bottom of the slope. It felt as if the little hatchback was a counter in a giant game of snakes and ladders as it edged its way up the hill again and again, only to be sent sliding back to where it had started.

After the fifth attempt, he turned to Adele. 'I don't suppose the ever-organised Adele has snow chains hidden away in the boot, does she?'

She gave him a look. 'We live in London, Nick. When do we need snow chains? The snow only gets a couple of inches deep and the school kids are lucky if it hasn't disappeared by lunchtime.'

'I was only asking. You do seem to have the uncanny ability to whip tweezers, Sellotape or a mini first-aid kit out of your handbag whenever required. I was wondering if the same magic worked with your car, that's all.'

'Making fun of me is not going to help.'

He put his foot down on the accelerator again, annoyed that she had taken offence at his attempt to lighten the mood. Why did she do that? Why did everything he said have to be a dig at her?

Once again the car began to slip and in his irritation he stepped too hard on the brake, and what in past attempts had been a gentle backward slide now became a fully fledged skid. As the slope flattened it was like being thrown off the end of a helter-skelter. The car shot backwards and, even though he regained some control, he didn't manage to stop the rear end banging into one of the very solid-looking gateposts.

'Nick!'

'I'm doing my best, Adele.'

She glowered at him and got out of the car to inspect the damage. Once again his best had fallen too far short of good enough. He got out and joined her. Apart from a large vertical dent in the hatchback door and bumper, it wasn't serious. It just wouldn't look very pretty until they got it banged out.

She held out a stiff arm and wiggled her fingers. 'Give me your phone.'

Seeing as he'd just pranged her car, he decided it wasn't wise to ask her to say *pretty please* before he handed it over.

She tapped in a number and waited, then, still not smiling, gave a thumbs-up sign that he presumed meant that his phone network had better coverage in this area and that somehow she'd managed to get a patchy signal.

'Hello? I need a tow truck or something to come and help us—'

Her brows drew closer together and she pursed her lips. 'Hello?'

A sinking feeling crept from his stomach right down into

his icy toes. He'd meant to charge his phone up again last night at Craig's flat, but there hadn't been an available socket while Kai had been straightening her hair, and then they'd got to opening a couple of bottles of beer and swapping stories…

Adele slapped the phone into his hand and stomped off to sit back in the passenger seat. His snazzy new mobile beeped pathetically and flickered into a coma.

He got back into the car himself, glad to be out of the thickening snowfall, and realised they didn't need to turn the heater up. Adele's anger was doing a great job of heating the air in the confined space all on its own.

'Classic Nick.' Her words were bare, but he knew the lava was bubbling out of control beneath the surface.

'Ah, come on! Even you can't blame the weather on me.' He grinned, hoping she caught the dimples he was flashing at her. He was in so much trouble now, it couldn't hurt to dig himself out any way he knew how. 'I know I'm good, but I'm not *that* good.'

'All we had to do was make a simple trip from London to Scotland, but you have to go and complicate the whole thing with your detours and your stupid navigation thingy.'

'That stupid navigation thingy stopped us going over a cliff!'

'Which we wouldn't have been anywhere near if we'd carried on on the main road instead of taking that turning.'

'Now, hang on. I seem to remember someone telling me to shut up and follow instructions.'

'I'm new to that thing. All it wants to do is get us back on the motorway, you said. How was I supposed to know it was going to take us on some wild-goose chase?'

'*Maaaaa.*'

Both Nick and Adele jumped out of their seats and stared at the sheep that was casually looking at them over the bonnet of the car. They looked at each other and back at the sheep.

It tossed its head and trotted off through a narrow gap between the gatepost and the dry-stone wall. Show-off.

'Wild-sheep chase, more like,' Nick said and rubbed his face with his hands.

When he looked at Adele, he could tell she was clamping her lips together in an effort not to laugh.

'Oh, for goodness' sake! You are impossible, Nick Hughes.'

'I know. I've had a badge made. "I am impossible," it says. I could have sworn I pinned it on my sweatshirt this morning, but it seems to have gone astray.'

One side of Adele's mouth curled up. 'You don't need a badge to state the flaming obvious, you know.'

He smiled back. No effort at dimples this time. Just a *pleased my wife has forgotten I'm the enemy* type of grin.

'I suppose it's not your fault. I mean, you couldn't have known it would take us down a farm track rather than a country lane, could you?'

Nick went very still.

Adele fixed her eyes on him. 'You couldn't, could you?'

He winced.

She flopped back in her seat and covered her face with her hands. 'It's done this before, hasn't it?'

'Only just after I'd first got it in the States. I kept getting lost in LA so I decided to invest in something to help. Then one weekend, when I had some time off, I went for a drive in the country. Ended up in an orange grove… But I thought it was just a teething problem, a bug that had worked itself out.'

She shook her head. 'A bug,' was all she muttered before she turned away from him to look out of the window. 'Just when I think I can rely on you at last, you remind me that I'm kidding myself. If I can't depend on you for the small things, how am I going to depend on you for the really important stuff?'

They sat in silence for another five minutes and twenty-three seconds. Nick knew because he'd become strangely absorbed in the clock on the dashboard. It ticked a steady beat in the silence, reminding him of a time bomb about to explode.

'Adele, can I have your phone, please?'

'No signal, remember?'

'I know, but I can walk to the top of the hill and see if I can get a signal there.'

'Don't be stupid, the light's almost disappeared.'

He held out his hand. 'Exactly why I should do this sooner rather than later. You don't want to be stuck out here all night, do you? If you think it's cold now, you should wait until three in the morning.'

She handed it over and crossed her arms over her chest. 'Just…be careful,' she said, staring at the floor.

He was about to say careful was his middle name, but thought better of it. No way was Adele buying that one. He could think of a ton of words she would use to describe him, and none were particularly flattering.

Adele watched Nick through the window as he trudged up the snowy slope. He was keeping to the grassy verge and it didn't look as if he was about to skate down the hill as the car had done. She turned her attention to the dials that controlled the heat in the car.

Even with the heater at full blast she could still see her breath coming in clouds and the tip of her nose was numb.

She shivered. If she'd been in London, she'd have thought she was dressed warmly in her jeans and nice thick jumper, but here in snowbound Cumbria she was feeling the need for more padding.

Layers. That was what she needed. More layers. And she knew just where to find them. Her suitcase was in the boot and she had a vest top and a long-sleeved T-shirt that would insulate her better.

She climbed out of the car, legs stiff from being cramped into a small space for hours and from the cold. However, her plan for layers was thwarted when she got round to the boot.

The big, fat dent was more than just an eyesore. The door was jammed shut and no amount of tugging and pulling and yelling at it made it budge. She knew that for a fact, because she tried all three. In the end she resorted to yelling on its own. Not very helpful, but rather therapeutic.

When she ran out of steam, she decided to have another go, more gently this time. As she pressed and pulled, she thought she heard the click of the catch. Exultant, she sank her fingers into the recess surrounding the button and pulled with all her might.

More yelling.

This time from fear as she toppled over backwards and shock as her bottom met cold snow. Very cold snow. And the freezing wetness spread with surprising speed, soaking the backs of her legs and climbing up her back where her coat had ridden up.

She floundered in the drift near the gate for a few seconds more then managed to pull herself to standing. If she thought she'd been cold before, she was seriously mistaken. This was plunge-into-the-deep-end cold—before she'd been merely paddling in the shallows.

She searched the horizon for Nick as she clambered back into the car, her jaw quivering, even though she was clamping her teeth together to stop them from chattering. He was nowhere to be seen. Probably over the brow of the hill and out of sight. Suddenly she felt very alone. She reached forward and turned the radio on for company. The signal was bad, but it felt good to hear a human voice.

Ten minutes later she was not only feeling isolated, but also worried. Surely Nick should have been back by now? What if he hadn't been looking where he was going and had fallen off that cliff? He could be lying there, surrounded by sheep, with a broken leg, too cold to call for help.

And they had no way of summoning assistance of any sort. The light was fading fast. Nobody would ever spot them out here. They hadn't seen a car for ages. Only that light travelling in the distance…

Light! She had lights. Maybe if she turned the headlights on, someone would see them.

She clambered into the driver's seat and twisted the switch on one of the levers. The headlights had been on half-beam anyway, but she switched them on to full beam and left them there. And then she had another bolt of inspiration. Stationary lights might just look like a lamp at a window, but flashing lights would surely attract attention.

She started flashing the full beam on and off at regular intervals and after twenty or so flashes she really hit her stride. Morse code. She remembered the signal for SOS from Brownies. Three short flashes, three long ones and three more short ones.

Please let someone be there to see them! And not just sheep baa-ing at the pretty lights.

She kept it up faithfully for another few minutes then gave herself a rest. The sun had set and the flakes were falling in large round blobs. A tinge of icy blue remained on the horizon, but very soon it would be pitch dark and Nick might never make it back here.

She started flashing the headlights again, randomly this time, as much to guide him back to the car as it was to be a beacon to someone else. Nick had to come back. He couldn't leave her alone again. Not like this. And more than that, she couldn't bear the thought of him cold and wet and injured in the darkness.

Yes, he drove her to distraction sometimes, but there was a big difference between wanting him out of her life and him not having one. She could cope with the split if she knew he was somewhere else on the globe, doing what he loved, but if he was gone for good...

Her heart began to gallop and her breath came in puffs, steaming the windscreen. When a knuckle rapped on her window she almost shot through the roof.

CHAPTER EIGHT

'IF YOU suggest we get naked and cuddle up to conserve body heat, I'm going to slap you.'

The twinkle in Nick's eyes was enough. She wanted to slap him anyway. Perversely, she also wanted to strip off and cuddle up to him. Freezing temperatures obviously affected logical thought.

'I mean it, Nick.'

'I know you do.'

Yet his eyes twinkled all the brighter. Impossible man.

'How on earth did you get this wet staying in the car, Adele?'

She rolled her eyes. 'I was trying to get warm.'

'By lying down and rolling around in the snow?'

'No, by trying to get some extra clothes out of the boot. I'm not completely daft, you know. The door was stuck and I fell over trying to open it.'

Nick looked towards the back of the car then, before she could say anything, he launched himself through the gap between the front seats and clambered onto the back seat.

'Nick!'

'You didn't think of doing it this way?' He lifted the flap on the parcel shelf and reached into the boot.

'Um…no.'

Most of Nick's arm disappeared as he rummaged around. He then pulled out the travel blanket and first-aid kit she always kept in there. Next came his holdall, but he continued to wrestle with some unseen thing in the dark recesses of the car.

'Nope, can't shift it.'

'My case?'

He removed his arm and sat back on the seat, panting. 'Let's face it. It must have been a struggle to get a monster that size into that tiny space in the first place. The dent in the rear of the car has it wedged fast. I can't even undo the zip.' He winked at her. 'And you know what that means.'

'I am *not* sitting here naked! I'd die of hypothermia.'

'Sweetheart, if you don't get out of those wet jeans hypothermia is more of a threat than you might think.'

'Really?'

'Denim is one of the worst things to wear in this kind of weather. It soaks up water and takes a long time to dry. And staying dry is the d in cold.'

'Pardon?'

'C-o-l-d. Basic knowledge for climbers and walkers. Keep *clean*, avoid *overheating*, dress in *layers* and keep *dry*.'

'You know all this stuff from climbing?'

'Of course. You don't think I hang off mountains by my fingertips without making sure I'm safe, do you?'

Actually, she did. Nick never talked about safety lines or c-o-l-d or stuff like that. All his tales involved daring risks and near misses.

'Well, I wasn't planning to be out in this kind of weather. We should have been close to Invergarrig by now.'

He reached forward and stroked her arm. All the indignation melted away. She might like to blame Nick for a lot of things, but falling in the snow had been her own stupid fault.

'You do have to get out of those jeans—and anything else that's wet.'

Her mouth crumpled into a smile. 'It's a pretty poor way to get to see me in my underwear, you know.'

He grinned back at her. 'Hey, I can take it. After four years of marriage, I'm well aware that small, frilly things are in the minority in the underwear drawer. I've seen those big grey knickers you wear to the gym, remember?'

'They are not grey. They're pale blue—at least, they were once,' she said, starting to laugh.

'I've got clean clothes in my bag. You can borrow a pair of my jeans and a T-shirt and pullover.'

'Have you got any boxer shorts? The snow soaked through my jeans and even my underwear is wet and cold.'

He closed his eyes for a second and she watched his shoulders tense. 'Are you trying to get me all hot and bothered?'

She shook her head, but inwardly wondered whether she should be nodding. What was wrong with her? This was the worst possible time to start flirting with her soon-to-be ex.

'It's not going to work, you know,' he said, unzipping his bag and hauling a few items from inside. He reached in again, pulled out a pair of soft cotton-jersey boxer shorts and threw them in her direction. 'Eh, who am I kidding? I always used to think it was kind of sexy when you used to steal these to wear in bed with one of those little strappy tops.'

She tried not to smile, she really did. But she remembered the times when Nick had discovered the theft of his underwear and vowed to reclaim them no matter what. There had been lots of giggling and chasing and eventually, yet not surprisingly, lots of kissing.

Life with Nick might have been unpredictable, but it had been fun and she was surprised to discover she missed that part of their relationship more than she would have thought.

She hadn't realised how little she'd smiled in the last nine months until Nick had barged his way back into her life. Of course, she'd also cried and fumed and wanted to bang her head against the wall a lot more in those six days too, but somehow that didn't seem to outweigh the sheer pleasure of sharing a joke with him.

'You'll have to climb into the back to get changed.'

Adele looked at the tiny space around her. 'I can manage here fine, thanks. Pass me those jeans.'

Since her own jeans were wet and clung to her legs, it was no easy feat to remove them in the passenger seat. Even though she wasn't that tall, she found her knees and elbows bumping into all manner of things. What made it worse was that, even without looking, she knew Nick was wearing an I-told-you-so grin from where he sat in the back seat.

'OK, I admit defeat. I'm coming back there,' she said, pulling her jeans over her hips again, but not bothering to do them up. 'But I want you in the front seat and your eyes facing straight ahead.'

'Anything you say, ma'am.'

Adele wiggled her way through the gap in the front seats and somehow ended up sprawled across Nick's lap.

'Well, isn't this cosy?'

He didn't have to look quite so pleased with himself, did he?

'Front seat. Now.'

Nick manoeuvred himself so she was sitting on the seat and he was leaning over her. She did her best to ignore all the crazy sensations racing through her body, but to have him this close, brushing past her, was more than she could take. Just the proximity of one slightly rumpled but rather delicious man was raising her body temperature quite nicely. A few seconds more and steam might start to rise from her damp clothes.

Just as he was easing his legs through the gap to climb into the front seat, there was a moment when they came nose to nose. She held her breath and willed her eyelids not to slide closed.

Nick had stopped wriggling and he was looking right into her eyes. The cheeky twinkle was gone, replaced by a quiet longing. Not lust, not even desire, but something far more dangerous. He wasn't just looking at her wet hair and soggy clothes. He was looking at *her*, the woman underneath those things, and she could see that it was the person inside he ached for.

His eyes darted downwards to look at her lips and she couldn't help but return the gesture. Those lips that were so often curved into a roguish grin could also be soft and serious. Her tummy tingled at the memory of what they were capable of.

And then he was gone. The rest of him slipped through the gap and he was in the passenger seat. He tapped the rear-view mirror with his finger so it faced downwards—a very chivalrous gesture. The sort of thing she'd always wanted him to do in the past.

But now, as she sat alone in the back seat, all she felt was disappointed, no matter how stupid it was to think that way. Part of her wanted him to take a cheeky peek. Before this whole separation thing he would have done that. And although she'd scolded him for behaviour like that, she'd always liked the fact that he just couldn't seem to help himself.

Only now things were different. Now she was…resistible.

And suddenly she realised that she didn't like it when Nick did as he was told half as much as she thought she would.

'What was the deal with the headlights while I was fruitlessly standing on top of the hill trying to get a signal?' he asked, still staring straight ahead.

She hurried into the dry clothes then clambered back into the front to show him, repeating the series of long and short flashes that had made up her mayday message. 'It was a daft idea, really. I just thought flashing the lights might draw some attention to us.'

'I didn't know you knew morse code.'

She turned to look at him, studying his face. 'I didn't know you did either.'

They stayed looking at each other, half-smiles on their lips. Nick flicked the radio off then moved to turn down the heater.

'Don't do that! It's cold enough in here already.'

'Adele, we've got to. We've got the light on in here, you've been using battery power to flash the headlights, the radio was on…if we're not careful we'll have no power left at all.'

'Oh. I didn't think of that.' No, she'd been too lost in the moment, going gooey-eyed at her husband.

'There's a good chance we're going to have to stay here all night and we need to conserve the power. I suggest turning the engine on and using the heater for about five minutes every half an hour, just to stop it getting any colder. When it gets light we can hunt for a farmhouse or something, see if we can use a phone or get a tow up that hill.'

Such frighteningly good ideas. Just when had Nick got so practical?

'But I'm so cold already.'

He gave her a wry smile. 'You were on to something when you mentioned cuddling up for warmth. Why don't we get into the back seat, put our coats and the blanket over the top of us and see if we can keep each other warm?' The smile turned into a fully fledged grin. 'I promise to keep my clothes on if you do.'

She tipped her head to one side and smiled back. 'I promise.'

'Rats.'

Adele scooted along the seat until she was pressed against the door, giving Nick ample room to clamber into the back again, but he dived out the passenger door and re-entered the car through the rear one on the same side. Adele turned to stare at him.

'Why didn't we just do that earlier instead of clambering over these seats?'

'Ah, well,' Nick said as he patted the seat beside him and held the blanket open for her to climb under. 'There's a very good reason for that.'

She shuffled along to huddle under his arm and made sure she was facing outwards a little—just for her own safety and peace of mind. 'And the reason is…?'

'It would have been a hell of a lot easier…' he dropped a kiss on top of her hair '…but not half as much fun.'

Adele shook her head, glad he couldn't see the naughty smile creeping across her face. 'You're—'

'Impossible. I know.'

Nick's breathing seemed deep and even. Adele lay against his chest, feeling it rise and fall. They'd been sitting like this for almost two hours and, as the glow on the horizon faded, they'd been plunged into pitch darkness.

The only light was from a small torch she kept in the car for emergencies. She had it grasped in her hands as if it were a talisman of some kind.

Despite the fact her torso felt fairly warm, her fingers and toes were like tiny blocks of ice. She blew on them, still gripping the torch, but as soon as the moist cloud of her breath had evaporated, her fingertips were just as cold as they had been seconds earlier. She tried not to let it, but a hard lump of fear settled inside her.

They were miles from anywhere and it was snowing so hard now that the windscreen was completely covered in a couple of inches of snow. Only the side-windows gave a glimpse of the blackness outside.

She didn't think she'd ever been this cold before. It seemed to penetrate her skin and invade her very bones. A quiver ran through her and she huddled a little closer into the warm body next to her.

'Are you OK?'

She turned to face him. 'I thought you'd fallen asleep.'

He curled his arm around her a little tighter. 'No, just conserving my energy.'

'I'm scared, Nick.'

He didn't say a word, no joke about turning into giant snowmen or anything, and Adele knew it was serious.

'We're in trouble aren't we?'

'We could be. It depends on all sorts of things: how long the petrol lasts, how much charge there is left in the battery, how close we are to a main road or a farmhouse.'

The fear spread from her tummy into her arms and legs. She grabbed on to the tiny flicker of an idea that popped into her head. 'We saw a light though, didn't we?'

He stroked her arm in long, rhythmic sweeps. 'We did.'

But his voice told her it didn't mean anything.

Suddenly she couldn't sit there like that, just waiting for the cold to numb her to the point of no return. She jumped up and lunged forward through the gap in the front seats and waggled the lever for the headlights frantically. The torch clattered on the floor.

'Adele!'

He tried to pull her back, but she batted his arms away. 'We've got to try, Nick! We can't just sit here and give in. We've got to take control, do something.'

'I know.'

He let go of her and then she felt a blast of icy air as he opened first the rear door and then the one right next to her. A firm hand clamped down on hers and held it fast, stopping the frantic flashing of the lights.

'Adele, let go. We *are* taking control. We're conserving the fuel and the battery and we're keeping ourselves warm and dry. There isn't anything else we can do. We just have to sit tight.'

She stopped trying to push against his hands and looked at him. He seemed so big, so solid, so sure. And then she realised that all the heat they'd saved was rushing out the open door and that he was getting colder and icier by the second as he filled the door frame.

She pushed past him and climbed into the back seat again, pulling the blanket round her.

'I'm...I'm sorry. I don't know what...'

He got in beside her, grabbed the torch out from where it had rolled under the seat and pulled her close. His cheek was icy against hers as they wrapped their arms around each other.

'I've just undone all the good we've done over the last couple of hours, haven't I? I've wasted the battery, let the cold air in and...look at you.' She reached up and brushed away the snow caked into his hair. 'I'm sorry. I just didn't know what to do.'

He hugged her tighter. 'It doesn't matter. But you have to listen to me.'

She nodded, hearing her hair rustle against her ear as it was trapped between her head and his shoulder.

'Sometimes you just have to accept that you can't control things. Stuff happens, no matter how much you plan. And when it does, like now, you just have to keep your head and do as much as you know to keep yourself afloat.'

'But that's the problem!' Her voice sounded all high-pitched and nasal. 'I don't know what to do.'

'But I do. I've prepared for being stuck in this kind of weather on my climbing courses. You've got to trust me.'

She pulled away and looked hard at his face, distorted as it was by the upward beam from the torch. 'I do trust you.'

He lifted his free hand and held his thumb and forefinger an inch or so apart. 'About this much?'

She smiled—something she'd thought had been frozen out of her—and nudged his thumb a little wider. 'Maybe this much.'

Everything went dark as he flung his arms around her and the torch beam danced in the opposite direction. 'It's going to be OK. *We're* going to be OK. I promise.'

She sank into him and stayed there, breathing the scent of him in and feeling safer than she had done in months.

'What time is it?' It seemed as if they'd been trapped in this frosty cocoon for weeks, as if the snow had bleached out all sense of time and reality.

Nick lifted his arm to look at his watch and she snuggled into a more comfortable position, arms curled in front of her and her legs across his.

'About quarter past eight.'

'And what time will it get light?'

He exhaled. 'Not sure. It'll be a bit later than in London, because we're further north. Seven? Seven-thirty?'

Neither of them said it, but she reckoned they were both thinking that was an awfully long time to wait. And the temperature was sure to drop further.

Nick laid his head on top of Adele's and held her tight. Panicking like this…it just wasn't what Adele was all about. He'd seen her lose her temper and get frustrated when things didn't go according to plan, but he'd never spotted that look that had been in her eyes just now. He hardly knew how to define it.

Not panic, although she was certainly scared, more like confusion and hopelessness. And that scared him. Adele always had a plan, was always focused on where she was going.

He just hoped that it was the shock of being a couple of

hundred miles away from her comfort zone and not the early stages of hypothermia. Disorientation was normal if that was the case. He lifted his hand away from her shoulder to tuck the blanket in even tighter behind her and anchored it down with his hand when he was finished.

If she was already getting hypothermic, it wouldn't be a tow truck he'd be calling first thing in the morning, it'd be an ambulance. And a night in the car was not going to improve their situation in the slightest.

He moved slightly to look down at her cuddled against his chest. Her eyes were closed, although she wasn't sleeping. Was it terrible that, even though they were in the worst pickle they'd ever been in, he felt a strange glow deep inside that she needed him? It felt good to be the one in charge for once.

Half an hour ticked past on the dashboard clock and Nick stirred. Adele complained as he pulled away.

'I'm just going to turn the engine on for a few minutes and get a bit more warm air circulating.'

Rather than opening the door and losing any residual heat, he climbed into the front of the car and turned the key they'd left swinging in the ignition. The sound of the engine seemed deafening after the snow-muffled silence.

Warm air—not hot, just warm—drifted from the heating vents. The fans were making some awfully strange noises. It almost sounded like voices far off in the distance. He shook his head. Wishful thinking. Now was definitely not the time to descend into his fantasy world.

He was just about to reclaim his space next to Adele when a loud thump on the window made him jump out of his skin. Attacking sheep? Adele lurched forward, eyes wide, then screamed as a face appeared at the window only inches from her own.

The face disappeared for a second and he heard a muffled shout. 'Jeff! Jeff! I've found 'em. Over here.'

Then the door was opening and a large light swung around, dazzling him. He turned the engine off and opened the door, too dazed to think about leaping out and working out what the heck was going on.

Once he was on his feet he came face to face with a sturdy-looking farmer.

'Just as well you turned the car over when you did, young man. We'd have gone straight by you if you hadn't.'

Adele emerged from the rear of the car, looking small and frightened. He moved over to her and put a protective arm around her shoulders as a second man came into view.

'How did you know to look for us?' he asked the man he presumed was a local farmer.

'All in good time. First, let's get you and the missus some-where dry and warm. My Land Rover's just the other side of this gate.'

And then he produced the one thing that would have made the whole nightmare unnecessary—the key to the padlock. The two men must have jumped over the gate to get to them.

Once inside the cab of a seriously ancient-looking farm vehicle, the farmer explained.

'Harry Smith,' he said, introducing himself. 'My grandson is staying with me and when he told me a couple of hours ago that someone was signalling SOS from the fells, I told 'im he was soft in the head. But sure enough, about an hour later he saw it again and he called me to come have a look. I got Jeff and we came out searching.'

Adele smiled weakly. 'You saw my SOS?'

'Sure did.'

Nick's heart dropped. Despite all his good planning about keeping them safe and warm, it had been Adele's frantic sig-nalling that had saved them in the end. So much for saving the day and being the rock his wife could depend on. Once again, Adele had rescued herself, and pretty pleased she was looking about it too.

Ten minutes later they drew to a halt outside a grey stone farmhouse. Harry nipped out of the Land Rover and had a brief conversation with a woman silhouetted in the open door then returned to usher them inside.

'You two come in and have a cup of something hot and Della will get a room ready for you.'

'Thanks a bunch, Mr Smith,' Nick said, helping Adele out of the back of the car. 'You must be wondering how we came to be stuck shivering on your farm.'

Della bustled them inside and provided mugs of steaming cocoa while Nick relayed their sorry tale. By the time he'd finished the farmer's wife had returned and was beckoning them.

'We don't want to put you out, Mr Smith,' Nick began.

'Harry—please.'

'You said you've got family staying and we don't want to turn you out of your beds. Adele and I can stay down here on the sofa in front of the fire if that helps.'

'No problem, is it, Della? We turned one of our outhouses into a holiday apartment a couple of years ago and Della's been across to make the bed up and turn the heating on.'

'Bed?' Adele squeaked and Nick elbowed her firmly in the ribs. They were safe and warm and she'd been perfectly happy to snuggle up half an hour ago. They'd just have to share.

He wasn't about to let Adele go into 'hotel-mode,' as he called it. Every time they had stayed anywhere she'd always got niggles about one thing or another. Perfectly adequate mattresses were declared too lumpy and the toast at breakfast was always too overdone. How on earth was the cook supposed to know that Adele liked her toast so lightly done that it should merely be waved in the general direction of the grill?

Harry led them outside and across a yard to a square stone building with a heavy-beamed door. Inside was surprisingly cosy. There was a small sitting room and kitchen on the lower level and up a curling flight of stairs was a bedroom with *en suite* bathroom.

Fluffy towels sat on the end of the bed and the duvet looked about a foot deep. Nick felt sleepy just looking at it. And before he knew it, Della and Harry had disappeared and he and Adele were standing alone in the room, either side of a huge brass bed, staring at each other.

CHAPTER NINE

ADELE picked up a towel and clutched it to her chest for protection.

'I'm going to have a bath.'

Nick nodded. 'Good idea.'

Why was it so awkward, standing in a bedroom with her own husband? Anyone would think they were strangers.

He was looking back at her, a strange expression on his face. 'It's not going to run itself, you know.'

'What?'

'The bath. Even if they'd invented such a thing as a self-filling bath, I doubt they'd have them installed deep in the Lake District...' He drifted off and his gaze wandered and fixed itself somewhere to her right.

She smiled. 'You're trying to work out how to build a self-filling bath, aren't you?'

He grimaced. 'Is it that obvious?'

She dug her fingers into the soft loops of the towel she was holding and nodded, her head bobbing only slightly. Pure Nick. His brain was always ticking over on some scheme and, while she'd been frustrated at the way he had become so absorbed in his work, forgetting everyone and everything, she loved the way his mind worked. It was quick and creative, always coming up with something unexpected.

Look at the way he'd handled their situation earlier. He'd been marvellous, taking charge and looking at the problem rationally while she'd been flipping out.

Her gaze drifted down to her feet. How embarrassing. He'd never think of her as Super Adele again now. She glanced up at him.

'I'd better go and…'

And she shuffled into the bathroom and closed the rough wooden door behind her.

The bath was fantastic. One of those roll-top ones with clawed feet that was so deep she'd be able to submerge herself right up to her eyeballs if she wanted. And, boy, did she want to. Not only was she cold, but she was also dirty from her fall in she snow and stale from the car journey.

Suddenly the idea of having clean, smooth skin smelling of the mineral-scented bath oil sitting on the shelf was the stuff of her wildest fantasies.

She peeled off her coat and hung it on the back of the door. But when she turned to face the tub she got a shock.

You have got to be kidding me!

There, sitting a couple of inches from the plug-hole, was a big, fat, hairy spider. It skittered forward then stopped. Eyeing her up, probably. In all likelihood, it was a distant cousin of the one she'd evicted from her bath last week and he'd come to satisfy the family honour.

She clenched her hands and took a deep breath. She'd done it once; she could do it again.

But the spider must have sensed her fear—the way horses or dogs could—and as she took a shaky step forward, it also advanced. She was very tempted to cry. It had been the day from hell and all she wanted was a nice, warm bath. Why did the universe taunt her in this manner?

She backed off and sat down on the closed toilet seat.

Not today. She couldn't do it today. Her nerves were already too frazzled.

What she was about to do was completely pathetic, but she didn't care any more.

'Ni-ick!' she yelled.

He came charging through the bathroom door and skidded to a halt. 'What's wrong? Do you need a doctor?'

She bit her lip and raised her eyebrows. Only a head doctor.

'No. There's a...' she waggled a hand instead of saying the word '...in the...' More hand-waggling. 'Do you think you could...?'

Nick grinned. Two hundred watts and full dimples. What on earth was he looking so pleased about? Probably enjoying her moment of weakness.

She hugged the towel even closer to herself and sighed as he picked the spider up in one deft move and disappeared back into the bedroom. Moments later she heard footsteps on the stairs and the front door open. She shuddered just thinking about it.

To rid herself of the memory, she turned the taps on and started undressing. She folded Nick's pullover and the T-shirt she'd worn underneath it and placed them on a little wicker-seated chair in the corner and had just removed her bra when the door creaked.

She grabbed for the towel and covered her front with it.

'I've evicted the trespasser, so—' He stopped in his tracks, muttered an apology and backed out of the room.

How ridiculous was this? They were married, yet behaving as if they were prudish teenagers. Why did it matter if Nick saw her naked? He'd seen her that way countless times before. All she knew was that somehow it did matter and that it wasn't a grown-up, mature decision, but something in her subconscious setting off alarms about vulnerability and self-protection.

She dropped the towel, still aware of Nick in the next room, then continued to undress. At least the bath soothed some of her tension away. When she emerged, she was as pink and fresh and sweet-smelling as she'd dreamed she'd be.

Unfortunately, there was no clean, fresh nightwear to slip into, just Nick's T-shirt and boxer shorts. Funnily, she didn't mind. The T-shirt was soft and warm and smelled a little of him. It made her feel safe in a way she avoided analysing.

She opened the bathroom door gingerly. Nick was lying on the bed, hands behind his head, legs crossed, staring at the ceiling. He turned his head as the door creaked wider.

'Feeling better?'

'Much.' She fidgeted with the hem of the T-shirt. 'It's all yours, if you want it.'

He swung himself off the bed and landed with a jump. She moved away from the door, giving him plenty of space, and slid quickly into the closest side of the bed. Funny how she automatically picked the right side. Her side. After months of forcing herself to sprawl in the middle of the bed, her body hadn't forgotten what it was like to sleep close to him.

Try as she might, she couldn't drop off, even though her bones ached with fatigue. She started to doze a couple of times, lulled by the sound of the shower from the next room, but there was an annoying thought buzzing like a fly at the back of her brain. Nick would soon be climbing into bed with her and this awareness prevented her from tumbling headlong into the sleep her body was desperate for.

They hadn't shared a bed in almost a year and it seemed bizarre that what had once been so natural, so intimate, now seemed awkward and artificial. If she'd been any more exhausted, she'd have started crying at the thought, although she'd have been hard-pushed to explain why.

Instead, she rolled over onto her side, facing into the middle of the bed and away from the bathroom door, and closed

her eyes, blocking the escape route of the tears that threatened
to bulge over her lashes and spill down her cheeks.

The sound of running water stopped and she tensed.
Moments later the door opened and she heard him pad round
the bed. The mattress dipped as he sat on the edge. And then,
for ages, he didn't move and she wondered whether he was
watching her. Pretending to be asleep would be childish,
wouldn't it?

With great effort, she parted her lashes and sneaked a look.
He was blurry, but still utterly gorgeous, all damp and clean
from the shower. He smiled at her, a soft upturn of his lips
that was totally heart-melting.

'Hi.' The smile grew.

She opened her eyes wider. 'Hi.'

She wanted to speak as they stayed there looking at each
other, but there wasn't a sensible word to be found in her
head—never mind ready and waiting on the tip of her tongue.

He lifted the duvet and climbed in. He smelled as good as
he looked. Would it be a complete giveaway if she dragged
the scent of him in on a deep breath? Probably. And then he
would smile even more and she would blush and the whole
thing would be even more awkward.

She closed her eyes again and let the breath out instead,
her sigh ending in a tiny shudder.

'Still cold?'

His voice didn't need to rise above a whisper they were so
close and his words warmed her cheek.

'A little.'

It was true. Della had turned the heating on, but the holiday
cottage must have been empty for months and, although it was
warmer than outside, the room was still a little nippy. Even
the crisp, clean bedlinen was a bit chilly.

Nick lifted the duvet slightly with his arm, making a space
just the right size for her. She hesitated.

'Come on. You said it yourself. Combined body heat and all that.'

He was right. Just being practical again.

Practical.

Odd, how quickly she had got used to applying that word to him. Less than twenty-four hours ago she would have scoffed at the thought of anyone calling him just that. Free-spirited, maybe. Impulsive, definitely. But never practical.

However, a lot had happened since the alarm clock had rung this morning and she was seeing a whole new side to her husband. And this wasn't something that he'd developed since they'd been apart. He fell into the role too easily and it was obvious that it had always been there. So why hadn't she seen it before?

Not that she wasn't pleased. She was. It was just there was another emotion creeping below the surface and, when she hunted for a name for it, she discovered it was guilt.

This was her doing. Right from the very start of their relationship she'd assigned him the role of the fool—a lovable, impossible joker. She'd never let him prove himself otherwise and in the end he'd embraced the part, fulfilling all her expectations. She'd never given him the space, and she'd certainly not treated him like the equal partner she expected him to be.

She focused on his face and realised he was still waiting.

'Hurry up. My arm's getting tired.'

She rolled onto the other side so she was facing away from him then scooted backwards until they were only just touching. He lowered his arm and the duvet enfolded her. She tucked it under her chin to stop the cold air snaking in.

It was so familiar, the way they fitted together—his arm circling her waist, her foot gently crossing over his ankle. It was more by instinct than decision that she'd shuffled into position.

'Don't worry,' he said, close to her ear. 'I'm not going to pounce on you. You can trust me to behave.'

Her eyelids drooped and she nodded ever so slightly. She could trust him—with anything, with everything. And she was too exhausted to explore the vague sense of disappointment that accompanied his words.

Ditto.

A fog descended on her brain as her muscles relaxed and she moulded even further to him.

If she'd been any more alert, she might have been worried about the fact that, as she sank into a deep sleep, the last thought in her mind was that this was where she belonged.

All Nick was aware of at first was warm, soft skin in contact with his own. All the energy seemed to have bled out of his muscles during the night and, although he mentally planned to move a limb or two and heave himself out of bed, the actual ability to do just that eluded him.

As his brain came more into focus he realised it wasn't just the fact he didn't have the strength that was keeping him from getting out of bed. He just didn't want to move. Simple as that.

He'd be crazy to move even a millimetre when he was wrapped around a woman as unique as Adele. She looked so peaceful, her breathing soft and shallow, her silky hair tickling his nose. But it was more than her beauty that fascinated him. It was her strength, her fire, all her contradictions.

He placed a tiny kiss on the bare skin of her upper arm and she let out a little murmur of pleasure. He'd been so angry with her for months after they'd first split up. He'd told himself she'd killed the love between them, but he would have been more accurate in admitting he hadn't *wanted* to love her any more.

In the end there had been no denying it and he'd turned

down a couple of prime jobs to fly across the Atlantic to see if he could win her back. He hadn't thought he could love her any more than he already did, but he'd been wrong. During the last week he'd discovered he loved her more than ever and he had a sneaking suspicion it was because now he understood.

The months apart had seemed like a punishment at the time, but hadn't they actually done him some good? When he'd returned, and had seen her with fresh eyes, he'd been astonished how blind he'd been in the past.

Now he could see not just the armour plating, but also the vulnerability beneath it. And he adored the wounded, soft-centred Adele more than he had her superhero counterpart.

By not jumping when he'd said jump, she'd shattered all his illusions about her and he should thank her for that. Their marriage would never have survived if they'd gone on the way they had been.

She wasn't a goddess any more; she was a real woman. Human. And he had to admit she felt very warm and human now as she nestled against him, stirring slightly as she began to wake.

Her eyelids flickered and, a couple of seconds later, opened. She turned her head then shuffled round a bit to look at him.

'What time is it?'

He checked his watch on the bedside table. It showed the time as just past seven, but the room was artificially bright as the pre-dawn light reflected off the snow outside and entered through a gap in the curtains.

'Five past seven, or thereabouts.'

'Is the sun up yet?'

'Not quite. It's magic hour.'

She closed her eyes and screwed up her forehead. 'Magic *what*?'

'Hour. Magic hour.'

'Feels like death-warmed-up hour to me.' She opened her eyes again and shifted back a little so she could focus on his face. He made very sure she didn't drift too far away.

'You're not making any sense, you know,' she added.

He chuckled. 'It's a film-making term. Not so much a whole hour, but two half hours around sunrise and sunset when the light has a unique quality. It's an in-between time. Night blends into day. They're two complete opposites, but when they meet something wonderful happens.'

Adele's mouth stretched wide into a yawn. 'The cold got to you yesterday. You're rambling.'

'I've never made more sense.'

She snapped her mouth closed and looked at him.

'You and me, Adele. Two opposites. But when we get it right something wonderful happens. Something magical.'

He raised himself onto one elbow to look down at her. His wife. How had he been so stupid as to nearly let her get away? Stupid, stupid pride. But she was here now, her large brown eyes getting darker by the second, and he was going to make darn sure he didn't lose her this time.

He bent his head and brushed his lips against hers. Only a whisper of a touch, but it set him alight. He didn't wait more than a fraction of a second before he kissed her again, this time savouring the soft plumpness of her lips.

She made an *mmm* sound in the back of her throat and pulled him closer. He couldn't help himself. He had to touch her. One arm was trapped under Adele, but with his free hand he explored under the hem of her T-shirt—his T-shirt.

Oh, who cared?

He kissed down the length of her neck as she stretched her head back and arched underneath his touch. But then a thought occurred to him, and he couldn't swat it away, no matter what Adele's hands were doing. He broke apart from her and she opened her eyes, puzzled.

'Adele, I…'

The skin between her brows wrinkled.

'I just want to know that you really want this—and not just because you're sleepy and aren't thinking straight. The last twenty-four hours have been pretty surreal and I don't want to do anything you might—'

She pressed a delicate finger onto his lips. It took all his will-power not to take it into his mouth and consign the rest of his sentence to eternal silence.

'—regret,' he managed finally.

She moved her hands to either side of his face and stroked his temples, his eyebrows with her fingertips. The look on her face brought a lump to his throat.

'Nick.'

She said his name as if it were a precious secret, and he knew her answer.

Before he could dip his head to kiss her again, she laughed and gave him a shove, sending him crashing backwards onto the mattress. Then he saw her face smiling, coming up close and going out of focus as she swung a leg over his body and leaned in to kiss him.

Once upon a time, he'd described Adele as icy. Many people made that mistake, but they just weren't paying atten-tion. From a distance, the shimmering brilliance of frost and extreme heat looked almost identical.

Adele kissed him again, her hands exploring his body, causing little fires to ignite round his toes, and soon he was too busy experiencing the flames to analyse it any further.

When Adele thawed like this things got very hot. White hot.

Adele opened and closed cupboard doors, looking for mugs. A food basket sat on the kitchen counter, filled with tea, coffee, milk and the most mouth-wateringly soft white bread she had ever seen. Della must have left them the food basket last night when she'd made up the beds, but both she and Nick had been far too tired to even notice it.

Nick.

Her heart did a little lurch just at the thought of him.

Despite the warm afterglow that made her insides feel like melted butter, there was also a little fluttering feeling in the pit of her stomach, a sense of uneasiness. A warning she should be very, very careful.

She'd made love with Nick. And boy, it had been way-off-the-scale, thermometer-popping fantastic, but now she was starting to wonder if she'd lost her mind. This had the mark of a one-night stand—a moment of madness. She'd told Nick she wouldn't have any regrets but, even though she'd meant it at the time, she suspected it had just been wishful thinking.

But at the same time, this *wasn't* a one-night stand. It was Nick. And it had felt like coming home, not like meeting a stranger. Oh, this was so confusing!

She slumped into one of the wooden chairs surrounding the hefty pine table and supported her head in her hands. However, she didn't get the chance to think her way out of the dilemma as Nick came crashing down the stairs and burst into the kitchen.

She stood up again, mouth halfway open and ready to say goodness knew what. He scooped her up in his arms and peppered her face with kisses.

'Good morning once again, Mrs Hughes.'

Her mouth opened a little further before he cut her off again by rapping on the pine table in the middle of the room, a wicked glint in his eye.

'How sturdy do you think that kitchen table is?'

Despite the furnace that immediately *whoomped* into life inside her, she gave him a weak smile and extracted herself from his arms.

'Coffee?' was all she could squeak out.

He looked slightly perturbed, but recovered quickly

enough. 'Good thinking. We're running on empty. Best get some fuel in us first.'

She turned to fill the kettle and he draped himself over her shoulders and nuzzled his chin into her neck. If he kept this up she was going to go stark, staring mad.

'Why don't you pop across to the farmhouse and see if Harry will give us a lift back to the car and directions back to the main road while I sort out…fuel?'

Nick was definitely back in Labrador-mode. He bounded out of the kitchen door and she heard him whistling as he crossed the farmyard.

What had she done? In momentarily lowering her defences this morning, had she agreed to a reconciliation? Nick seemed to think so. Somehow, he'd forgotten all the things that had driven them apart in the first place. There was so much to sort out in her head. Having sex hadn't blasted all of those things into oblivion. They were still there—like a tribe of warriors on the horizon, waiting to charge down the hill and hack away at this moment of euphoria.

Nick had hurt her so badly when he'd left last time. She didn't think she could bear to go through all of that if it didn't work out a second time. She had to think of herself, of keeping herself safe.

And he still didn't know about the miscarriage.

But now was not the time to tell him. How could she crush his mood with something like that? But she was going to have to say something, to set a few boundaries.

Maybe, just maybe, they still had a future together, but it was going to take time to repair the holes they'd ripped into each other. This time they needed to plan it all out and build on a proper foundation. And if Nick wasn't going to agree to that, they were dead in the water before they'd even started.

CHAPTER TEN

SHE was safe from Nick's attentions while he had his hands on the steering wheel. It gave her time to work out what she wanted to say. After that he might not be so enthusiastic. At least she'd managed to distract him from the kitchen-table idea by sending him off to use the Smiths' phone to call Invergarrig and explain the delay to his mum.

Maggie had been frantic, of course, and when they'd got back in range of a mobile-phone transmitter, both their phones had erupted in a symphony of beeps from text messages and missed calls.

The dent in the back of the car wasn't nice to look at, but hadn't caused any major damage. Harry had even managed to unwedge her case. After being fussed over by Della, they'd said their goodbyes and driven off, Adele navigating from the list of directions Harry had scrawled on the back of an envelope. So much for high-tech wizardry.

She looked at the hamper of food in the back seat that Della had insisted they take for the journey. She'd even dried Adele's clothes for her before they left, for which Adele was very relieved. She seemed to be able to think better when she was wearing her own underwear.

Nick had promised Harry and Della they'd return in the summer for a proper holiday and hadn't seemed to notice that she hadn't joined in making plans. She had to say something to him now, before it all got way, way, way out of control.

She stared ahead at the road. The sun was out and, as they left the hills of the Lake District behind, the snow was thinning. At this rate they'd reach the hotel by mid-afternoon.

Nick grinned across at her. 'This evening is going to be a piece of cake now.'

'It is?' If anything, she was dreading it more than she had before. At least then she'd had it all figured out. She'd had a strategy to follow.

Trust Nick to relish the flying-by-the-seat-of-his-pants approach. Mind you, he pretty much lived like that all the time. She was surprised his jeans hadn't sprouted wings before now.

'Now we don't have to pretend to be happy together—we are. We can just enjoy ourselves.'

Right. She had to say something now, before she ended up being back with Nick by default. This had to be her decision too. She just couldn't be swept along by his enthusiasm this time. Too much was at stake.

Nick sensed Adele had something she wanted to say about two minutes before she opened her mouth. It was something about the way she breathed, he decided, as if she were rehearsing something in her head and breathing at the gaps in the unspoken sentences.

There was no point pushing the issue and asking her what was up before she was ready, because that only caught her on the hop and she got flustered. She had to have that perfect opening line. The best plan was to keep his eyes on the road and wait.

Sure enough, before the next junction, she cleared her throat.

'Nick?'

'Yes.'

That's right. Keep the tone casual. Do nothing to put her off her stride. If she lost her train of thought, she might sink back into silent muttering. And, if that happened a few times, she'd give up altogether and then he'd never knew what she'd been going to say. It would drive him nuts for days.

Maybe, if he'd employed these tactics more frequently in the past, instead of cracking a joke to ease the tension, things wouldn't have reached boiling point and they'd never have spent all this time apart.

'I think we need to clear something up.'

Oh?

He raised his eyebrows, but said nothing, because he really wanted to hear this.

'It's about last night…well, this morning…sort of.'

So much for the perfect first line. She must really be in a stew about something.

'Such as?'

'Give me a second…'

He concentrated on overtaking a lorry while she regrouped. She clasped her hands into a tight little ball.

'I'm not sure we can just jump into being back together.'

What?

'But you…we…'

'I know. And I'm not saying it wasn't good—'

'You're telling me it was a one-off? For old times' sake?'

'No!'

'Then what? Do you want to give this marriage another go, or not?'

'That's just it. I don't know.'

Oh, she really knew how to make a guy feel good about himself.

'It's not that I'm saying no, Nick. Just that we haven't solved anything. Sleeping together hasn't made all our problems disappear, has it? We've still got to face all the things that kept us apart and then, when we have, we'll need to think about whether this is what we really want.'

Translate that into: Adele needed to think about what she really wanted. His mind was already made up.

'Fine.'

'Nick, I—'

'Do you mind, Adele? It's getting busy now we're approaching Glasgow. I think I need to concentrate on driving for a bit.'

'But—'

She snapped her mouth closed and stared straight ahead.

It had been childish of him to axe the conversation like that, but he'd wanted to show her she couldn't just have it her own way all the time. And she wasn't the only one who needed time to think.

Concentrating on the traffic calmed him. For the next twenty miles he mulled over what she had said. He should have seen it coming. Adele didn't do spontaneous. Then he remembered the way she'd practically pinned him to the bed that morning and let out a low whistle.

OK, *sometimes* Adele was spontaneous, but he knew that most of the time she needed space to sort things out. You couldn't just dump things on her. She needed time to adjust and refocus.

That was why she'd flapped and squawked about his job in LA when he'd made his big announcement. He'd just been so excited he hadn't stopped to think. Of course, Adele would have freaked out. Now he'd stopped being angry with her, he could see the whole situation more clearly.

If he'd given her a little more time, she'd have probably come round to the idea. After a couple of days he'd have found her on the internet, researching cheap flights and checking her workload. She'd have had all sorts of brainwaves about how to make it work. She was great at planning details. Only he hadn't given her the chance.

Well, this time it was going to be different. He would give her as much time and space as she wanted. He would talk about whatever she wanted to talk about. And just to make sure things went his way, he was going to be as charming as he could possibly be at the party this evening. He wasn't going to give her any excuse to give in to her fears and bail on him a second time.

'OK. Point taken. What do you want to discuss?'

There was a long silence. At least, it seemed long. She hadn't been expecting that.

Eventually she said, 'I think we need to clear up the whole argument over your Hollywood job.'

'You're right. We need to resolve that.'

He could feel Adele looking at him. 'Nick, are you feeling all right?'

'Fine. Never been better.'

'Well…OK. Let's talk, then.'

It wasn't the easiest thing, having an in-depth discussion while driving, but the more of this they thrashed out before the party the better. He dived right in, hoping she'd appreciate him taking the lead.

'I know I really upset you when I left, Adele, and I'm sorry for that. I was just so cross with you I wasn't thinking straight.'

'I was cross with you too.'

'Sweetheart, I don't think anyone's going to disagree with you on that one.' He wondered if she'd ever replaced the plates from their dinner service.

'I expected you to go down the pub, come back later and make a joke out of the whole thing like you normally do. I was in shock when I realised you were halfway across the world.'

'I think I was in shock, too. I couldn't believe I'd done it either. I tried to phone when I landed, didn't I?'

He glanced across and she was blushing. 'Yes. You did. And I slammed the phone down on you.'

'You needed more time to calm down. I should have realised that.'

'No, Nick. Don't put it all on yourself. I was having a temper tantrum, plain and simple. But I was scared. Seeing you only in dribs and drabs until there was nothing left of our relationship but long-distance phone calls and strained reunions was more than I could handle. I didn't want to get to the point where we didn't know each other any more.'

Exactly what had happened with her parents and, although she pretended not to care, he knew it still hurt her deeply. The hole their daughter had left behind in their lives had been quickly filled with business trips and jet-setting, and when Adele had gone to stay with them she'd discovered that whatever 'home' had been had evaporated.

That was why buying a house and investing time and energy in it had been so important to her. He'd been daft to assume she wouldn't baulk at leaving her beloved nest with practically no warning.

He got that.

What he didn't get was why she decided to jump before she was pushed. Why not even try to make the relationship work? He'd hoped he was worth more to her than that.

'I know I sprang the whole thing on you and expected you to jump on board as quickly as I did, but I did it so we'd have more time together.'

She humphed. 'Being on a different continent means we spend more time together? I don't see how.'

'Think about it. I've worked with Tim Brookman, Oscar-winning producer famous for his action flicks. My name is well and truly on the map. I've had so many job offers since finishing the film I can't count them. Rather than me chasing the jobs, now they're chasing me.'

'Well, that's all fine and dandy for you, but how does that help me? I'd still be stuck in our little house on my own most of the time.'

'I can cherry-pick the good jobs now—ones that pay well—so I can take longer breaks, or projects closer to home. And I have a plan I want to share with you.'

'A plan? You?'

'I've been thinking about teaming up with Andy and opening our own special-effects studio. We could do a lot of the construction in our own premises when we find somewhere and the two of us could share the travelling. In a few years, if things get more established, we could employ a couple of film-school graduates, train them up and send them off to do some of the leg work. I could stay behind and run things from this end.'

'A studio? That's a fantastic idea!'

'I know.'

She smiled at him. 'Just look at where engaging your brain before you rush into things can get you. Mind that car.'

He hadn't realised he'd taken his attention from the road for that long. He slowed to increase their distance from the car in front.

'So you like the idea?'

'I do. It could be a roaring success.'

But there was still a hint of wariness in her voice.

'So, do you understand why I had to take the job? Why it meant so much to me—to us?'

'Why didn't you tell me all this *before* you left?'

He sighed. 'The studio was only half an idea at that point and I know how much you hate half-baked plans. Anyway, you know what we're like when we get on a roll with the arguing. Rational explanations tend to go out of the window.'

'It makes more sense to me now I know that, but at the time

it just seemed as if you wanted me to uproot myself and abandon my business, my friends—everything that made me feel safe and secure. I felt threatened and I lashed out.'

'Don't I make you feel safe, Adele?'

She took too long to answer.

'Well, that says it all, doesn't it?' he said. 'You'll go out on a limb for Mona or your other friends, drop everything for them when they need you, cheer them on at every hurdle. Why can't you do that for me too?'

He really shouldn't have opened this can of worms. They were going to be coming off the motorway soon and winding Scottish country roads were not the right setting for this discussion.

'I do—at least I try to.'

'Well, maybe I want more. Maybe I want you to open up to me the way you do to Mona. You tell her everything, but there's a part of yourself you won't share with me, no matter what I do. Somehow you just can't trust me enough. And I don't think we've got any chance of success if we're not going to be totally open and honest with each other.'

She didn't move. Her hands were folded in her lap and she was very still.

'Throw me a crumb, Adele? For starters, you were very vague about why you refused to return my calls when I was in the States. You can't have been sulking for a whole nine months. What did I do that upset you so much? I can't fix it if I don't know. I've said my piece, made my explanations. I'm ready to do whatever it takes to fix our relationship.'

She shook her head.

'Tell me why you were so angry you decided it was easier to walk away and ask for a divorce. I know I was stupid, but I need to know what it was that I did that hurt you so badly. You're always saying you want me to take things seriously. Well, I'm not wisecracking now, am I? Talk to me.'

'It's not that…'

He took a quick look at her. She seemed on the verge of tears.

'I can't talk about this now, Nick, and you need to concentrate on the road. We'll talk later, OK.'

It was a statement, not a question. Subject closed.

Once again she'd slammed the door in his face. How was he ever going to get through to this woman? He'd been so optimistic this morning, but now he was starting to worry Adele had been right when she'd said they had a lot to sort through before they could have a future together.

The drive to Invergarrig went a little way to calming Adele's nerves. They took the road that passed by the side of Loch Lomond and stopped in the tiny village of Luss to eat the packed lunch Della had made them.

The roads were lined with tiny little stone cottages and, in the February air, smoke rose from almost every chimney. The sun was low and everything seemed to be tinted yellow and grey as they walked down to the small beach on the shores of the loch and sat on a bench to eat their sandwiches, a Thermos of soup and home-made cake.

Nick wasn't saying much, but she could hardly blame him. She'd chickened out, big time.

Honesty truly was the only way forward, but laying it all out there for him—her fears he'd walk away if she proved less than perfect, the miscarriage—meant she was giving up the one thing she had left: control. If she opened up to him, spilled her soul out at his feet, he'd have all the power. And, if he chose to leave her a second time, she'd wither.

Let's face it, she told herself. She'd only been hanging on by a thread last time.

But then again, if she didn't open up now, she might lose him anyway. If only she could be sure. She needed guarantees that it was going to work this time.

Nick's voice interrupted her shilly-shallying. 'Do you want that?'

She looked down to the remaining half a sandwich on her lap. Thick white crusty bread with slabs of cheese and chutney. It looked lovely, but she couldn't face any more of it.

'No. You go ahead.'

She stood up suddenly. 'I'll be back in a sec. I need to make a call.'

Nick had no option but to shrug his agreement as his mouth was still full.

She wandered along the shore and checked her mobile. There was a signal—just, but it got stronger as she moved towards the tourist shops near the wooden jetty.

She pressed the speed-dial button to call Mona's number and let it ring.

'Hello?'

'It's me.'

'Hang on a tick…'

She could hear Mona's muffled instructions to Josh to colour in nicely while Mummy was on the phone.

'OK, you got me. What's the news from Scotland? Have you brained the ex with a haggis yet?'

Adele chuckled. 'He's not technically my ex, Mona. And, no, I haven't resorted to using offal as a weapon.'

'Too bad. What's the boy wonder got to say for himself, then?'

She sighed. 'He wants to give it another go.'

Mona made a sound that was halfway between a grunt and a snort.

'He says it's going to be different this time.'

'They all say that, Adele. They always have rational, reasonable excuses for their bad behaviour then make you feel awful if you don't buy into them.'

'I know, I know, but he is different…or maybe it's me that's different. I can't tell.'

Mona's voice softened a little. 'Just be on your guard. A leopard can't change its spots, even if it swears blind it can. Even if it wants to. Don't you remember how he made you feel?'

Frustrated, irritated and ready to scream. But, when things were good between them, life had been exciting. She'd felt sexy and wonderful and treasured. The bottom line was: Nick made her happy.

'No, I haven't forgotten.'

'That leopard of yours can be very charming when he wants to be, Adele. Don't be blinded by it. See what is really underneath, that's all I'm saying.'

For the first time ever, she thought she really did.

'OK, I'll be careful. Take care, Mona.'

She so badly wanted to trust her instincts, but what if Mona was right? What she was experiencing with Nick right now wasn't real life. It might seem new and exciting, but how long until the whole thing seemed old and tired again?

'Ring me again if you need moral support, OK?'

'OK.'

'Bye.'

Adele said goodbye and hung up. She looked down the beach to where Nick was. He had finished his lunch and was skipping stones on the loch's surface. Part of her longed to join him, to giggle and cuddle and wander back to the car arm in arm, but she didn't know how to break through the glass wall she'd built between them.

Mona's words had set off a chain of thoughts she wasn't sure she wanted to deal with. Was this reconciliation just wishful thinking? Smoke and mirrors? She wished she knew. Real marriages couldn't be patched up with a little digital trickery.

Nick would always believe that a little tweak here, a little glue there, and most things could be fixed. It was what he did best. But some relationships, once broken, were broken. She knew that for a fact.

Nick succeeded in skipping a stone a record amount of times and punched the air in triumph. He was so full of fun, full of life. No wonder she'd felt hollow all those months without him.

And she knew one thing for certain: she didn't want to feel that empty again.

She wandered over to him and waited for him to throw the last of the stones in his hand.

'Nick? Why did you come back? To England, I mean.'

He looked at her, a sense of weariness in his eyes.

Don't make me say it, those eyes said. Don't make me say it if you're not prepared to give something back.

'You know why I came home, Adele.'

He turned and walked off in the direction of the car park.

Home, he'd said. He'd come home. Not to a house. Not to bricks and mortar and fancy handles on the kitchen cabinets, but to her.

Nick might have left, but he'd also come back. A concept she was so unused to, it had taken her a week to cotton on to the reasons behind his return. He wanted her back.

She inhaled sharply. He'd always wanted her back. Only, at the time, all she'd been able to feel was the sting of his departure and she'd responded the only way she knew how— by locking the door after him and pretending it didn't matter that he'd gone.

And, if she'd let him, he'd have turned up on the doorstep a week or two later, with his dimples and a big bunch of gaudy flowers and they'd have sorted it all out.

She picked up a smooth, flat stone and tossed it in the direction of the loch. It hit the water and gurgled its way to the bottom.

Nick was right; she'd been shutting him out of her life in

one way or another the whole time she'd known him. He was asking for more. He deserved more.

She could see Nick far ahead of her, opening the car, and, after he'd swung the door wide, he paused and turned to look at her.

She was going to give him more.

But she'd never been one for ripping the plaster off in one go. She was just going to have to do it in stages, dismantle her barriers bit by bit. And the first thing she was going to have to do was to let him know that she wanted him to come home too.

It was almost three-thirty by the time they reached Invergarrig. The main road into the town ran down the side of Loch Garrig and over a crumbling humpbacked bridge. As they went over the top they could see the spires of Invergarrig Castle through the trees. It was like something out of a fairy tale.

The town was nestled in a sheltered bay where the water was dark and flat. A small patch of mist hung over the water.

The town itself was charming. Whitewashed stone houses and shops with identical black doors and windows lined the main street. In fact, all the buildings in the main part of the town followed the same design, including Loch Garrig Hotel, where the party was to be held.

Maggie Hughes had insisted they all stay there for the weekend on the grounds that there just wasn't room for a crowd of fifteen children and grandchildren in her little three-bedroomed house.

They parked in the gravel car park out front. Adele couldn't help feeling a pang of sadness at the battered state of her little car as she grabbed her handbag, eased herself from the passenger seat and followed Nick inside.

They walked past a large lounge on their way to the reception desk. A noisy game of charades was going on. Children were squealing and adults were cheering and booing.

Debbie, Nick's middle sister, spotted them first and added

to the squealing herself before running over to them and enfolding both of them at once into a big, squeezy hug.

The noise from the lounge stopped. At first she heard gasps and then running feet and pretty soon she and Nick were in the middle of a rugby scrum. Being licked to death by a whole pack of puppies couldn't have been more terrifying—or more wonderful.

They were dragged into the lounge and forced to tell the story of their nightmare journey. Thankfully, Nick left out the early-morning details, although she wouldn't have put it past him to make a cheeky reference. He and his sisters seemed to tell each other everything.

Nick finished their tale and the conversation moved on to family news and anecdotes. Someone brought Adele a cup of coffee and she sat back in her comfy armchair, the warmth of the log fire tickling her cheek, and let the noise and laughter flow around her.

What a difference from her infrequent audiences with her own parents. There was no awkwardness or long silences. She'd never even heard her father crack a joke.

This family was wonderful and she was privileged to be a very small part of it. The only niggle was that sometimes she felt Nick's sisters didn't know how to take her. She wasn't good at the easy banter and, although she found it easy enough to be physical with Nick—too easy, if this morning had been anything to go by—she always found it a little awkward being *touchy feely* with other people. The hugs always seemed to be too tight and last a little too long.

But the Hughes family knew how to pull together and love each other when needed. They knew how to support each other and trust each other and share with each other.

Nick had only been four months old when his father had left for good and his mother and sisters had doted on him to compensate for the lack of a father figure. She'd seen photos of him when he was little. He'd had it even then. Charm by the bucketload. And he'd known it too, by all accounts.

His sisters, Charlotte, Debbie and Sarah, seemed to be able to forgive him anything. 'It's just Nick,' they would sigh and laugh when he did something impulsive and daft.

He's not a little boy any more, Adele had wanted to scream sometimes, but it would do no good. He would always be the darling baby boy, even when he was collecting his pension. And just for confirmation of her theory, there was the eldest, Charlotte, across the room, ruffling his hair after he'd said something cheeky.

Adele took another sip of her coffee and gave a little sigh.

OK, it ruffled her feathers to see them treat him like that but, deep down, she was a little jealous. She'd never had anyone to fuss over her: cheer her on when she was doing well, wipe her tears when she wasn't.

And then Nick had come along and done all those things for her, even when she'd refused to let him. Hadn't he brought her champagne whenever something went well at work? He'd listened to her drone on about business plans and staff problems. He'd always been a reassuring shoulder for her.

And yet she hadn't seen it.

Or at least, she only remembered the negative side. Such as how he'd seemed unfazed and calm in the early days of her consultancy business when she was a nervous wreck and sure it was going to fold. She'd wanted him to wail and beat his breast with her. But he hadn't. And the small seeds of resentment and disappointment had been sown.

He'd been solid and calming when she'd ranted about the things that had seemed so important at the time. She couldn't even remember what all the fuss had been about now. What good would it have done if he'd joined her in her bellyaching? Instead of doing what she'd wanted, he'd done what she needed: he'd been her rock.

He'd always been her rock and somehow she'd thought he was quicksand. So much for the woman who always thought she had all the answers.

Nick's mum worked her way round the room and perched herself on the edge of the armchair after Adele rose to give her a kiss and a quick squeeze.

'How are you feeling, Maggie?'

'Fighting fit.' Adele saw the tiredness in her mother-in-law's eyes, but hadn't expected any other answer.

'Sounds as if you had a bit of an adventure on the way up here,' Maggie said. 'In more ways than one, but I'm glad you came, Adele. I know it can't have been easy for you.'

'Um.'

Her heart skipped into a faster rhythm. Nick had said he hadn't told his mother they were having problems. How did she…?

'I appreciate you taking time off from your business to come all the way up here. And, of course, for sharing Nick so soon after he's got back from California.'

She was safe?

'Thanks, Maggie. You know I wouldn't have missed your party for the world.'

Her mother-in-law nodded and fixed her with an uncannily shrewd look. 'I know.'

Adele smiled, but she felt it was a thin disguise. Maggie was one of the sharpest women she knew. All of a sudden, it seemed a tad optimistic of Nick to think his mother hadn't read between the lines and guessed something was up between the two of them.

Then came the question she'd been dreading.

'Living apart for so long can't have been easy. How are you and Nick getting on these days?'

CHAPTER ELEVEN

NONE of the truthful answers to Maggie's question would do. The most honest thing to say would have been, *I don't know.*

'Great,' she finally answered and increased the wattage of her smile to a more convincing level.

Maggie tilted her head and looked at her. 'Really?' she said softly.

Adele nodded, her head bobbing, smile fixed.

Her mother-in-law's concerned expression was chased away by a broad grin. She rubbed Adele's arm and gave her another kiss on the cheek. 'I'm so pleased. Good for you.'

Adele might have noticed Maggie's slightly odd response if she hadn't been so relieved she was no longer under the spotlight. She breathed out a sigh of relief.

First hurdle over—and probably the hardest. This evening, everyone would be too busy having fun to take a good look at her and Nick. It gave her a bit more time to screw up her courage and do what she knew she had to do to save her marriage.

Nick caught her eye and motioned to the lobby.

This was escape time. They could slide away and settle in their room and hide out until the pre-party drink in the hotel bar at six. Maggie had the whole event organised and time-tabled with military precision. Adele was tempted to fall at the woman's feet and worship.

She excused herself and walked towards him as he held his hand open for hers. It felt so natural, letting her hand slide into his and walking slowly from the room, their arms swaying gently between them.

Maybe things weren't quite right at this second between her and Nick, but they had been great in the past and maybe they could be great again. Better even.

It was almost a wrench when he broke contact to accept their room key from the receptionist. He handed it to her.

'You go up and have a shower or something. I'll go and get the bags.'

Adele did just that, and when she stepped out of the bathroom, rubbing her wet hair with a towel, her case was perched on the end of the bed.

She half expected him to be lying on the bed waiting for her, as he had been the night before, but the covers were un-rumpled and Nick was nowhere to be seen.

'Hand me that XLR lead, will you?'

Nick held out a hand while still crouched behind the decks for the sound system. Dave, the local DJ his mum had hired, placed the required item in his palm. Nick connected the lead, stood up and wiped his hand on the front of his jeans.

'Thanks, mate,' Dave said. 'I thought I wasn't going to get set up in time. You've been a real help.'

'No problem. It was good to have something to keep me occupied.'

He gave Dave a little salute and wandered out of the moderate-sized function room.

He did his best thinking when he was connecting things, building things. Somehow, that kind of manual task occupied the bit of his brain that always got in the way when he was trying to work things out. And, let's face it, he had some pretty big plans to work out.

Winning back your wife was a little bit trickier than connecting leads or bolting things together. There were no blueprints when it came to love. He'd put all the pieces in place, done everything he could, and still he was getting no results.

He'd done his best to be open with Adele, to show he was more of a grown-up than she'd ever given him credit for, but she was still holding back from him.

It drove him crazy that all he could do now was keep doing more of the same. He would have to be there for her, prove himself to her by being consistent. For a man more prone to pulling out all the stops and going for the big finish, it made him restless. He wanted glitter canons and fireworks and he wanted Adele to swoon into his arms like the heroines in the movies.

He couldn't have that, of course. Pushing her now would only solidify her defences further. He was just going to have to be patient. Which wasn't good news at all.

The music was pumping, the guests laughing and drinking. All in all, the party was going really well.

Adele felt the heat of Nick's arm across her back and the gentle grip of his fingers at her waist. Really well.

She'd been so busy being angry at Nick for so long, she'd forgotten what good company he was when she wasn't in a foul mood. He was such fun, and not in an overly loud, extrovert way, but just because he drew you into his laid-back world where it was easy to smile and feel warm inside.

He'd made her cry with laughter already. The old Adele would have had a grump about smudged mascara, but it didn't matter tonight. All that mattered was that she and Nick were here together and she saw more than a glimmer of hope for them.

They were good together. And tonight they were facing

the world as a team instead of pulling each other in different directions.

Nick's fingers loosened on her waist. She looked up at him.

'Don't go away. I've just got to talk to my "littlest" sister. Mum told me she and Martin are off early tomorrow morning and I don't want to miss her.'

She nodded and wandered over to the bar to put her handbag down. Invergarrig's hotel was small compared to the London hotels where she had business lunches, and the party had taken over almost the entire ground floor, filling the lounge, the bar and the function room, where something with a steady bass beat was playing.

The only people to have braved the dance floor so far were a couple of Nick's eight- and nine-year-old nieces, showing off their best moves. But the night was young and, since this was Scotland, the spirits were flowing. Shortly, they'd be joined by somebody's uncle doing his best John Travolta impression and little by little the floor would fill.

Adele leaned across and asked the barmaid for a refill. As she waited for the girl to uncork a new bottle of wine, she scanned the room. Nick was in the doorway that led to the function room, lit now red, then purple, then gold.

He was deep in conversation with his sister Sarah. He was closest to Sarah out of all of his sisters, there being only a couple of years between them. Nick reached into his jacket pocket and pulled out a fat envelope and handed it to Sarah. Her eyes grew wide and her hand flew up to cover her mouth.

Then she prised a corner open with trembling fingers. Whatever it was that was inside prompted a flow of tears. Sarah flung both her arms round her brother's neck and squeezed for what seemed like five minutes. Nick just clung right back, an oddly sober expression on his face.

Eventually, though, he whispered something in her ear

and they broke apart. He was chuckling and she was smiling through her tears. That was Nick's gift—saying just the right thing to break the tension when the atmosphere got too tense.

She felt her heart grow and swell as he walked back over to her, not taking his eyes off her for a second. Her husband was a wonderful man. Why had she forgotten that? Why had she let the doubts and criticisms cloud that truth?

Self-protection.

That was the only answer she was able to come up with. Although why she'd been so sure she needed protecting from Nick was getting harder to recall.

'Put that glass down and come and strut your funky stuff with me, Mrs Hughes.'

She shook her head, but let him drag her towards the blaring PA system anyway. Just as she'd predicted, it was starting to get crowded in there as the DJ strung together some of his best floor-fillers.

Although the song they danced to was up-tempo, Nick managed to keep contact the whole time. He didn't crowd her or do the daft stunts and dips some of the other men were doing just to prove they weren't embarrassed to be up there and dancing with their wives. He held on to her while letting her move in a way that was natural for her.

After four more songs, she pleaded for a break to catch her breath, using the excuse her mascara must be halfway down her cheeks, and headed for the Ladies'. When she entered, she found Sarah touching up her make-up. She was looking all puffy and the eyeliner pencil was going in anything but a straight line.

When she noticed Adele, she quickly pulled a tissue from her bag and dabbed at her eyes.

'Sarah? Are you OK?'

'Yes.' Sarah's face crumpled. 'No.'

'What's the matter? Was it Nick? Did he say something?'

Sarah blew her nose and shook her head. 'No. It's not Nick. Nick's been wonderful.'

This seemed to be the time for some physical contact. Adele looked at Sarah's hand, wondering whether she should pick it up and pat it.

'Then what is it? What's got you so upset?'

They sat down on the upholstered bench opposite the mirrors.

'I had a bit of a row with Martin. Over nothing, really. Something so stupid…'

'Hey. We all do that.'

Sarah looked shocked. 'Even you and Nick? You always seem so happy, so…perfect.'

Adele gave a wry smile.

Sarah sniffed. 'We've been under a lot of stress recently. We've just had our second cycle of IVF treatment.'

That explained why Sarah was the only one of Nick's sisters not to have added to the copious amounts of grandchildren yet.

Adele raised her brows and Sarah shook her head, unable to speak for a few seconds, then she gulped down a big breath and continued. 'I just seem to be angry with him all the time. Everything he does drives me nuts.' She shook her head. 'Really, I'm just angry full stop. It's not Martin at all. It's just the whole thing seems so…unfair! Does that sound really awful?'

Adele shook her head, not trusting her own voice at that moment.

'My best friend just got pregnant—and she's only been seeing the guy for a few months. She's not even sure if she wants it. How is that fair when I want it more…?' The end of Sarah's sentence was drowned out by the sobs she'd been trying to hold back breaking through.

Adele didn't need any prompting this time. She gathered

Sarah into a hug and held her tight. She knew how crushing that disappointment was every month when all the temperature-taking and ovulation-predicting had been a big, fat waste of time. How much worse must it have been for Sarah, with all those injections and all her hopes riding on just one try?

Sarah's breathing evened out and she pulled away. 'Hey, don't you start!'

Adele used the heel of her hand to swipe away the tears.

'Even my stupid cat is pregnant!' Sarah said, managing a damp smile.

They both sniffed and giggled and had another hug.

'So, enough of my woes. How are you and Nick?'

The word *great* was hanging on Adele's lips. She even started to form the right shape with her tongue.

'Not great, actually.'

Sarah's eyes practically popped out of her head.

'But tonight, you look so… You two always look so…'

'Appearances can be deceptive. Actually, Nick and I had been trying for a baby too.'

Sarah squeezed her hand. 'How long?'

'We tried for almost a year.'

'And…nothing?'

Adele bit her lip. She hadn't had to say the words out loud to anyone yet. Mona had been there; she hadn't had to have it spelled out. But Sarah knew something of the pain she'd faced and the temptation to tell her, knowing she wouldn't be judged, was overwhelming.

A rush of heat hit the backs of her eyes and her lip quivered.

'I had a…' The tears began to drop off her cheeks at an alarming rate, setting up a steady *plop, plop, plop* on the clutch bag resting on her lap. 'A miscarriage,' she almost whispered.

She heard Sarah gasp and felt her warm hand on her back, stroking, soothing.

There wasn't anything either of them could say and she was glad Sarah didn't even try. Well-meaning platitudes were her worst fear, one of the reasons she hadn't owned up to it at work.

When the worst of the tears were over, Sarah offered her a clean tissue from her handbag. Adele took it gratefully.

'Nick must have been devastated,' Sarah said, popping the fastener on her bag.

Adele's stomach bottomed out.

Sarah shook her head. 'It must have hit him really hard,' she mused, 'for him not to tell any of us. That's so not like him. And it makes what he did this evening even more special.'

'How so?' Adele knew she was fishing, but she just couldn't stop herself. Anything to veer the conversation onto a different course and off Nick's knowledge of her miscarriage.

Sarah patted her bag. 'Well, I guess you know for yourself how much this kind of thing can put a strain on a relationship. One of the reasons Martin and I have been so stressed is that we've used up all our savings. Try number two was our last attempt. Nick suddenly presenting us with the cash for another try was like a miracle.'

She laughed and her red-rimmed eyes shone. 'He said he couldn't think of a better way to spend some of his first obscenely big pay cheque. You've got one hell of a man there, you know.'

'I know.' Or at least she did now.

Sarah stood to leave. 'I suppose I'd better go and find Martin, tell him it's not the end of the world after all if he forgot to ask for diet tonic for my G and T.'

A laugh burst unexpectedly out of Adele's mouth. 'That's what the tiff was about?'

Sarah rolled her eyes. 'I told you it was stupid.'

Adele nodded. It was all fitting into place now. Hindsight truly was a wonderful thing. Just like Martin and Sarah, their own unsuccessful attempts to start a family had put their relationship under terrible pressure.

And instead of supporting each other, they'd both tried to pretend it didn't matter—he with his jokes, she with her nothing-touches-me routine—but underneath there had been strong currents pulling them apart. She'd been like a violin strung too tight, and all she'd been waiting for was one wrong note to cause it all to snap and warp.

And that final straw had been Nick's job offer.

It had never been about the job itself. Her logical mind had told her ages ago that they'd have found a way to make it work in the end. Hell, troubleshooting was what she did for a living. If she couldn't have sorted it out, she ought to have given herself the sack.

She called out to Sarah as her hand was on the door knob to open the door.

'Don't worry about Martin. Just make sure you go and talk to him, tell him how you're feeling. Don't keep it all bottled up.'

Sarah nodded and disappeared through the door.

The way she and Nick had done. She hadn't wanted to let him know how weak she felt. She was a successful business-woman, ironing out other people's troubles on a daily basis. It had seemed so pathetic that she hadn't been able to fulfil the role of a successful mother too.

She'd always had a sense that somewhere, deep down, she was useless and she'd done her best to make a mockery of that feeling, pushing herself to succeed, never giving in to weakness. But it seemed life was having the last laugh when she couldn't even do the basic thing her body was designed to do. All the business awards in the world weren't going to make a blind bit of difference.

But it was more than this, more than the stress of trying for a child, more than the one secret she was keeping from Nick. She'd never been very good at communicating her needs to him.

And now she had something really important to tell him. Something that shouldn't have been swept under the carpet all these months.

She was going to tell Nick the truth, not the Adele-sanitised version of the truth, but the whole truth, mistakes and inadequacies and fears included. If she didn't, the secret would fester until it ate her marriage alive from the inside out.

She walked back to the mirror and pulled her mascara out of her bag. Just on the point of applying the wand to her lashes, she stopped, put it away and pulled a tissue out of the box on the counter.

Carefully she wiped away the grey tear-trails, and even her lipstick, and then she straightened, looked herself sternly in the eyes and walked from the room.

Nick had just managed to extricate himself from the clutches of Great-Aunt Phyllis when he felt a tap on his shoulder. No! If he had one more kiss that smelled of Germoline…

'Just wanted to say thanks again, little brother.' Sarah waved her handbag at him. 'You don't know what this means to us…well, I suppose you do in some way. Anyway, it just feels as if a great weight has been lifted off us.'

She turned to smile at Martin as he joined her and planted a kiss on top of her head.

'No, I can only imagine what it must be like, but that's what family is for, right? Your pain is my pain…'

Sarah looked as if she was going to blub all over again. 'Come here,' she said, opening her arms wide.

Nick walked into the hug and gave her a squeeze.

'Don't forget you can talk to me any time if you need to—about…anything.'

He drew away, puzzled. 'Sure.'

He smiled after his sister and brother-in-law as they walked away, arm in arm. He hadn't seen them looking so relaxed together for ages. And then he spotted Adele, standing across the room, staring at him, her handbag clutched to her front in a protective gesture.

She looked different, softer somehow.

He smiled and she softened further, and suddenly he had the feeling everything was going to be all right. He didn't know why, just that somehow they were over a hurdle.

He walked across to her, tucked her handbag somewhere safe and led her back onto the dance floor. 'Now, where were we?'

She glided into his arms as if she belonged there. The music was softer now, slower, and she rested her head on his shoulder, saying nothing. They swayed gently together for ages. He lost count of the number of songs that drifted past. It was as if they were soaking each other up, making up for all the lost months.

He pulled away to look at her. She stared back at him, not smiling, not frowning. There was something new in her eyes and, although she looked weary, as if she'd given up fighting him, he began to get excited.

The shutters were finally gone. He felt as if he could see deep inside her, down into the core that had always been bolted and barred until now.

He lowered his head and the kiss they shared was sweeter and deeper and more toe-curlingly fantastic than any other they'd had together. They seemed to be saying hello and, in a strange way, goodbye. Whatever the difference was, it was magical.

When the kiss finished, they stayed forehead to forehead, still swaying gently to a song neither of them heard. And as the DJ began to put some livelier tracks on again, Adele whispered in his ear.

'Nick, I've got something important to tell you. I need to explain.'

'Explain what?' Who needed explanations? He rubbed his cheek against her silky hair. Where they were right now seemed just fine, thanks.

She took a deep breath. 'Something…everything.'

CHAPTER TWELVE

THEY walked up the stone spiral staircase to their room in silence. Nick grabbed her hand as it swung by her side, even though she was a step or two ahead of him. Somehow the feel of his hand was comforting. And right now she needed comfort. This was the most terrifying thing she'd ever done.

The spiral staircase seemed to go on for ever. She wasn't sure whether that was a good thing or a bad thing. Her heart was beating so loudly she thought it might rival the muffled bass beat drifting up from the dance floor.

When they reached their room, Adele turned on the lamps on the bedside tables rather than the overhead light. The soft glow was cocoon-like and she felt less exposed than she would have been by the cheerful brightness of the fixture in the centre of the ceiling.

She sat on the end of the bed and folded her hands in her lap.

Just remember how brilliant he was all those months the pregnancy test came up negative, she reminded herself. It'll be fine. Really it will.

Nick joined her and she swivelled to face him slightly. 'Nick…'

That was as much as she had prepared. Normally, she'd have spent days running an important conversation through in her head before she actually piped up. The first sentence was crucial. Once the first words were out, the rest just came tumbling afterwards. Of course, the conversation hardly ever went exactly as the dress rehearsals in her head, but that didn't matter. She'd been prepared, in control.

But tonight there had been no time and Nick had all the power. The future of their marriage rested on how he responded to her revelation. That sounded pretty dramatic, but that was how she felt.

He took her hands and looked into her eyes. The expression of empathy and concern on his face just made the knot in her tongue bigger.

'Adele, you can tell me anything. You know that. You can trust me.'

She nodded, her answering smile a thin line.

'In the car…earlier…you said you wanted to know why I wouldn't speak to you after you left.'

She looked in his eyes for reassurance before she continued and found it there.

'Well, you were right, at first I was sulking, but then there was a different reason.'

Nick's forehead wrinkled slightly, but his expression said it was still safe to continue.

'I don't know if you remember after all these months, but we only had a few days to go until I could take the next pregnancy test.'

He drew her to him and held her in his arms. 'I should have thought. You had to deal with that negative result all on your own. And I didn't even ask…'

She shook her head against his chest. 'No.'

He took her face in his hands and tipped her face up towards his. 'Forgive me? I was an insensitive—'

'No.'

'You won't forgive me?'

She shut her eyes, not able to face him when they were so close, but then made herself open them again. He deserved this. After all the years she'd hidden away from him, she had to look him in the eye, no matter how uncomfortable it was.

'The pregnancy test was positive.'

A flicker of a smile passed over his face, before the logical side of his brain worked out something was wrong.

'But…'

The hands cupping her face relaxed a little and pain registered in his eyes.

She was not going to look down. She ordered herself not to, even though she needed to blink to evict the tears clogging her lashes.

'I lost it, Nick. Our baby died at just six weeks.'

In an instant, he was off the bed and standing almost on the other side of the room. A dark cloud passed across his features. The room was suddenly ten times as chilly as her snowbound car had been. Adele felt her heart start to rip apart.

'And you never thought to tell me before now?'

She bit her lip. She had to look away now. His anger was more than she could handle. The tear in her heart widened, leaving messy, frayed edges that would be impossible to repair.

'At first, when the test was positive, I was so shocked I didn't know what to do. I thought you might have left me…'

'Don't be ridiculous! I wasn't leaving you when I got on that plane; I was just going to work. You're the one who decided it was over.'

She felt her teeth squeeze together. She was being attacked and there was only one way to respond to that.

'You got on a plane and went thousands of miles away without telling me. Don't say that didn't give me a little room for doubting your commitment!'

'Commitment? Hah! That's rich coming from you!'

She stood up, suddenly needing to be on the same level as him. 'I *was* committed! Who was there in the home, running the show, while you messed around with bits of metal in the shed?'

This was all sounding so horribly familiar. She could almost have this argument on autopilot.

'OK, I forgot to wash up a few times, but that's just peripheral stuff. Emotionally, I was one hundred per cent committed. But where it counts—' he patted the area of his chest covering his heart '—you were only ever half there.'

Adele felt as if she'd been punched clean on the jaw. She could hardly get the words out her lips were quivering so much in a combination of despair and rage.

'Don't you dare tell me that I didn't love you!'

He ran his hand through his hair and walked to the window. 'I don't know. I really don't. Before tonight I've never truly questioned it, no matter what stupid games we were playing.'

Her stomach lurched and rolled. She had a choice here. She could re-erect the armour plating and fight her corner, or she could smash the last of her defences to pieces. Only one of these options was going to save her marriage.

She walked over to him and he turned as he sensed her approach. She took hold of his hands. They felt as heavy as lead weights.

'I *do* love you,' she said, demanding eye contact from him. 'More than anything.'

The expression on his face was blank. 'Suddenly that's not good enough any more.' He dropped her hands and walked past her.

She couldn't move—actually physically couldn't move—as he crossed the room and walked out of the door.

Not good enough.

Adele sank into the armchair close by. Well, she'd known

it all along, hadn't she? He was right: she was a lame, emotionally crippled excuse for a wife. No wonder he didn't want her any more.

She walked over to the bed, kicked her heels off and slid under the covers. When the world crumbled around her, she thought she'd feel differently, that she'd feel...something. It was as if all her circuits had overloaded and refused to process what had just happened.

Her husband had just walked out on her and all she could do was lie here and stare at the wall.

When dawn came she gave up trying to sleep and threw back the covers. Her case was still sitting on the other side of the bed, where Nick should have been. She unzipped it slowly, her fingers struggling to do even the simplest of tasks.

She dressed in her jeans, boots and a thick pullover, put on her coat and headed outside. Despite the heavy snowfall in the Lakes, only the highest, most distant mountains were snow-capped here. The sky was the palest of pinks on the horizon and the loch was almost completely flat. The hotel was next to a quay with a stony beach beside and she worked her way down the stairs to stand on the pebbles.

She picked her way over the large, almost fist-sized rocks that made up the beach until she was standing right on the shoreline.

What was she going to do now?

The only plan she had been able to come up with during the long hours of the night was to go home and throw herself into her business.

Nobody had said it was a *good* plan. It was a bad plan. And it wasn't just a bad plan; it was a *recycled* bad plan. It was what she'd done last time Nick had left her. At least back then she'd been able to kid herself she could make it the centre of her life. That it could be the only thing that mattered. Only now she knew that wasn't enough for her.

Not enough.

Nick's words from the night before echoed round her head. She'd squeezed every last drop of her soul out of its hiding place and presented him with it last night and that had been his verdict.

She took one more look at the snowy mountains, their peaks glowing pinker as the sun rose. There was no solace here, not even with all this beauty.

She stuffed her hands in her pockets and made her way back to the hotel.

She tried not to look for Nick as she entered the lobby. Where had he gone last night? Where had he slept? In the space of a few hours she was right back where she'd been only a week ago, knowing virtually nothing about her husband's life and movements.

No one was up yet. The party had gone on into the early hours. She'd vaguely been aware of the diminishing noise levels throughout the night, although her ears had actually been straining for the sound of his shoes in the corridor outside their room.

She wandered into the lounge and sat there in the darkness, waiting for the rest of the world to start living again.

It was there Maggie found her, staring out of the window, some time later.

'Adele?'

Adele twisted her head to look at her mother-in-law. Focusing on her seemed such an effort.

'What are you doing up so early?'

She was too tired to think of a convincing excuse and, since the worst had already happened, she might just as well tell it as it was.

'Nick and I had a fight and I don't know where he is.'

Maggie turned towards the lobby then looked back at her. 'I saw him out there, a while ago. He said he was going to go climbing with his cousin, Simon. I assumed you knew all about it.'

Adele shook her head.

'He'll be back, darling. He used to do this when he was a little boy—run off and hide somewhere while he sorted his troubles out. He doesn't like anyone to see anything but his happy, sunny side.'

'He won't be back this time. At least, not for me.'

Maggie sank into the chair beside her and stared out of the window too. After a few minutes she said, 'I'm sorry about that. I thought this trip would be good for you both and instead my little plan backfired.'

'Plan?' Adele turned sharply to look at Maggie, then her eyes widened and her mouth parted as the penny dropped. 'You knew? About me and Nick?'

Maggie raised her eyebrows. 'I'm sixty-five, Adele, not stupid. I knew there was something going on. My Nick's not very good at keeping things under wraps, is he?'

Unlike me, Adele silently added.

'I thought some time together might help you two see what a good thing you had going and that you ought to give it another go.' Maggie looked as if she was going to cry, a sight Adele had never seen before. She put her arm around the older woman.

'It almost worked. You knocked some sense into me, at least. Only it took me too long to realise what I had, and by the time I tried to get it back it had already evaporated. I should have been honest from the start,' she added, mostly for her own benefit.

Maggie seemed to be able to make sense of what she was saying. 'Don't be too hard on yourself. You've changed a lot in the time that I've known you, and sometimes it takes something seemingly catastrophic to catapult us out of our comfort zone before we can grow.'

Adele managed a wry smile. 'You've got that right.'

'Sarah told me about the baby, Adele. I'm so sorry.'

She couldn't cry again, really she couldn't. Her throat was

too thick, so she just nodded her answer. Maggie pulled her closer and she laid her head on her shoulder—just the kind of gesture she'd always hoped her mother would make for her when she was upset.

She got a tiny glimmer of why Nick put so much stock in his family. She sighed. Too bad she didn't have much of a family of her own to put stock in. Her parents didn't count. Nick was all she had, and she'd blasted their family to bits just as effectively as if she'd taken a shotgun to it.

The journey home was uneventful. No jams. No snowstorms. No stupid detours. Adele turned the sat nav on for company, even if she ignored almost every instruction it issued.

She'd thought that the trip up here had been bad, but she'd been wrong. This journey, with the empty seat beside her, was the journey from hell.

One more overhang to get over and he'd be at the summit. Nick hauled himself up the rope to join Simon at the top of Ben Dubh. The view was stunning. The ancient mountains with the sharp tops weathered off them looked both lonely and beautiful at the same time.

Thank goodness they were finally at the top. He took a look at Simon, who grinned back at him. That was the thing about mountains. When you looked down from the summit, as he was doing now, you could see all the ridges and obstacles. The path seemed easy, but on the way up it was harder to see what was what.

You could be climbing towards a lump of rock, thinking you were almost there, but once you were over it, you realised there was more climbing to be done—and it was usually harder and more frightening.

Off in the distance he could see the sparkle of Loch Garrig and the black and white houses of Invergarrig on its edge.

Standing up here, could he get a little perspective on the bombshell Adele had dropped?

At first, he'd felt angry and betrayed and incredibly, incredibly sad at the thought that, for a few weeks, he'd been a father and he hadn't even known about it. He felt as if he wanted to grieve, but he didn't know how. And it had all happened so long ago. He felt another bolt of anger flare within him. Adele had robbed him of that too, as well as of hearing the news their longed-for child was finally on the way.

OK, he'd have only had the joy for a few weeks, but he might never have that opportunity again.

Add to that the fact that Adele thought so little of him. She couldn't even trust him enough to tell him she was pregnant and, more than that, had obviously thought he'd be as good as useless in helping her through the miscarriage.

If she'd told him, he'd have been straight on that plane. He'd have held her and gone to the hospital with her. Together they could have got through it. But Adele didn't want *together.* He was only a last resort. Useful for catching spiders and that was about it.

He kicked a rock hard with his climbing boot and watched it tumble and bounce its way down the mountainside until it was too small to see.

If only she'd let him be there for her. If only she could have said just once that she needed him, but Adele had proved with one last, grand gesture that she was never going to change. He was an outsider and he always would be.

As he and Simon descended, his thoughts turned to the months following their split.

He'd thought her perfect in every way when he'd met her. Bright, passionate, energising. He hadn't reckoned on the ghost of a little girl, desperate for love and acceptance, hiding under the surface.

But Adele wasn't perfect at all. The events of the last

year had blown that concept right out of the water. Although he'd wanted her to take down the barriers, he hadn't reckoned on the fact life was going to be a lot messier without them.

And, as he placed one foot in front of the other, he started to think, not about himself and his own wounded pride, but about the woman he now knew was nowhere near invincible and how on earth she'd made it through the nightmare alone.

He leaned against the low wall surrounding the tiny front garden and waited for the doorbell to be answered. The sun had just set and, in a rather random pattern, the streetlamps were popping into life.

The door swung open and the woman looked at him and bristled.

'Nick Hughes! I ought to smack you right into the middle of next Thursday,' she said, barely hiding her contempt.

'Nice to see you too, Mona. May I come in?'

The scowl intensified. 'Only because I can't afford to let the heat out talking to you with the door wide open.' She turned and marched down the hall and into the back part of the house. Nick followed, closing the door behind him.

'What do you want?' she barked as soon as he entered the kitchen. 'And don't you even think of using that stupid grin of yours on me.'

Funnily enough, he didn't feel the slightest bit like using his dimples.

'I need to talk to you about Adele.'

'Why? So you can break her heart a third time?'

He took a steadying breath. There was something about Mona that made his hackles rise. She was just so…bitter.

'I need to understand, Mona. And you are the only person I can ask. She tells you everything. I only ever get the crumbs.'

Somehow this seemed to appeal to Mona's warped vanity.

She sat down on a kitchen stool and handed the baby sitting in her high chair a rice cake.

'What do you want to know?'

No point in beating around the bush, so he launched straight in. 'Why didn't she tell me she lost the baby? I can sort of understand why she didn't tell me she was pregnant at first. Let's face it, Adele needs a long cooling-off period.'

Mona almost smiled at that. He took it as a sign to continue.

'I just want to know why she couldn't trust me.'

Mona laughed. 'Aside from the fact you're the biggest kid she knows?'

'I might make light of things occasionally, but that doesn't mean I'm immature. We all have different coping mechanisms, Mona. And at least I tried to patch our marriage up—twice now. And I wouldn't be here gearing myself up for a third try if I was the child you all insist I am.'

'All men are kids,' she muttered, but the verbal attack stopped, so he guessed he'd made his point.

'You've got to realise it wasn't a conscious decision not to tell you, not at first anyway. She was a mess, Nick. I've never seen her like that. She didn't go to work. The house was a state. Every time she saw Bethany she lost the plot. It was awful.'

He frowned. So much was starting to fall into place now.

'And when she told you the news you did…what? Support her? Comfort her? No such luck. You tell her she's not good enough.'

'I never…'

It didn't matter what he had or hadn't said. He was hearing his own words the way Adele must have heard them and he felt sick and angry all at the same time. Acting like an adult? Pah! He was fooling himself.

Mona gave him a long, hard look. 'Take that feeling and

multiply it by a hundred and then you'll be where Adele was back then.'

He took a while to let all of that sink into his imagination. 'Good grief,' was all he could say after a long pause.

'Exactly. So stop feeling sorry for yourself.'

'I'm not!'

'Give me a break. You ran off to lick your wounds, just like you did last time.'

'So, what do I—?'

He was cut off by an ear-splitting wail from the top of the stairs.

'Mummy! I've been sick.'

Mona jumped off the stool and raced out of the room. 'Hang on there, Josh. Mummy's coming.'

He waited for five minutes then decided Mona would probably want shot of him as soon as possible. He was halfway down the hall when he heard her coming down the stairs. She stopped at the bottom and he turned to look at her.

'I haven't got time for this, boy wonder. I've got my own mess to sort out. You'll just have to deal with yours.'

He nodded and opened the catch. Just as he pulled the door open, she called out to him.

'Nick?'

'Yes?'

'For what it's worth, I didn't think you had the balls to come back and have another go.' She shrugged. 'When I'm wrong, I say I'm wrong.'

He smiled as he closed the door behind him.

Coming from Mona, that was high praise.

Hazelford Farm, the sign said. Adele turned off the main road and followed a bumpy lane for about a quarter of a mile until she reached a quaint but rather neglected farmhouse flanked by a couple of low outbuildings.

This was where FX Designs had their main office?

She checked the slip of paper tucked into the road atlas on the passenger seat. *Hazelford Farm, Limpington, Kent.* She'd assumed it was going to be a commercial unit on the site of an old farm, not an actual farm, but this was the place. She was supposed to be meeting the managing director here at ten to discuss some areas of the business he felt needed attention.

If the premises was anything to go by, she was going to have her work cut out for her.

She was a little early as it had only taken thirty minutes to get out of London and find the place. No harm in having a wander around. She might as well get a feel for the site while she was here. Making the most of the property they owned was one of the items on the list the director's secretary had sent her.

The house was not as bad close up. In the summer, the wild flowers in the garden would probably spring to life, but it wasn't even March yet and, apart from a few snowdrops, everything was brown.

She ended up in the little courtyard of outbuildings that had probably once been stables or barns. How would she know? She was a city girl through and through.

These could be converted into nice little design studios, given the proper injection of cash. Large skylights in the sloping roofs would give wonderful light. A door was half-open on one of the buildings and she stuck her head round it, making sure the cows had left long ago.

Not bad. It was bigger than it looked from the outside and…

A flicker of movement in the far corner halted her mental planning. A man in a suit was standing with his back to her.

She coughed. 'Mr…?'

The name on the email had gone straight out of her head. In fact, she wasn't sure if there had been a name on it at all.

FIONA HARPER

Very unprofessional of his secretary. She would have noticed sooner if she hadn't been so preoccupied with shoring up her crumbling life.

He turned and the world lurched.

'Nick?'

He nodded. No smiles. No dimples.

'What are you doing here?'

'I'm the owner of FX Designs. I need your help.'

It wasn't much information, but it scrambled her brain all the same.

'Couldn't you have called someone else? This is all a bit…' Awkward? Surreal? Downright bonkers?

'I needed the best. You are the best, aren't you?'

That was what she told her clients.

'Professional help or personal help?' she asked, wanting firmer ground.

'Let's start with professional.'

She looked round the dusty cowshed and raised her hands in a question. 'I normally work with established companies, sorting out things that have gone wrong. Yours isn't even off the ground yet. If this is all some stupid prank…'

He walked towards her. 'I was worried you'd think that, and I almost just called you up to talk, but I felt I needed to back up what I wanted to say to you—to show you I'm serious about this.'

New, serious Nick was making her nervous. She picked at a fingernail as he came closer.

'OK. So you want to turn this place into a studio? Like the one you were thinking of building with Andy?'

'Spot-on. Andy's too far away. I wanted somewhere that was an easy commute into London.'

'For the film studios?'

'No. For you.'

'Me?' Surely that wasn't a squeak that had just left her mouth.

'Didn't the email say I had personnel problems?'

'Um. Yes.'

'That's because I did something really stupid.'

He was standing right in front of her now. She gulped.

'I let my pride get the better of me and I let somebody go that I shouldn't have,' he continued. 'I'm so sorry, Adele. Once again, I forgot to put myself in your shoes.'

She gulped again, this time to try to keep a lid on some very unprofessional feelings threatening to break through the surface.

He reached out and stroked her cheek. The look on his face was so tender.

'You had every right to be angry, Nick. I let you down. I'm damaged goods.'

'No, I let *you* down. You did what I'd been asking you to do all along and as soon as you bared your soul I threw it back in your face. Forgive me.'

He kissed away the tear that had broken ranks.

'I should have told you before, I just…'

'Shhh. I know. We both made mistakes. We defended our own positions instead of pulling together and working as a team but, from now on, it's going to be different.'

'It is?'

He smiled and his dimples appeared. 'I need a partner.'

'Because you sacked the old one?' she asked, daring the tiniest of smiles.

'No, I need the old one back. Seems I can't live without her.'

'I don't think she's functioning very well without you either. She needs you more than she ever let on.'

She pulled his head towards her and kissed him. She was tempted to show him how much—right here, right now. When they broke apart, he grinned.

'I know I'm the adventurous type, but even I draw the line at cobwebby cowsheds, sweetheart.'

'Cobwebs?'

Adele was out of there like a shot. Nick followed hot on her heels, laughing.

'Come and see the house,' he said, tugging on her hand. 'I've got a problem only you can help me with.'

'Oh?'

'It needs filling with a few children and I'm lacking the necessary equipment on my own.'

She stopped and let go of his hand. 'So might I be.'

He pulled her into a fierce hug and kissed her forehead. 'Spending more than a few days in a row together might help. How often was I called away to work at the crucial time of the month? And if we can't do it the old-fashioned way, we'll adopt or do the test-tube thing or grow them in a big old cabbage patch out the back here.'

He pointed to a neglected vegetable plot round the side of the house.

She looked up at him. 'I love you.'

He flashed his dimples. 'I *am* pretty wonderful.'

That deserved a punch on the arm. He got one.

'I surrender. I'll tell the truth—just don't hurt me any more!' Then his expression became more serious and he lowered his head and kissed her so gently it was like a whisper on her lips. 'I love you, Adele. Not Perfect Adele—she's a pain in the butt—but beautiful, feisty, brave you.'

Oh, no. She was back up on the pedestal and this time the height of it was truly terrifying.

Her face fell. 'I'm not brave. I'm a coward. You of all people should know that.' She had to make him see. Super Adele was gone—dead and buried—and she didn't want him worshipping a ghost.

He cradled her face in his hands and made her look at him. Then he kissed her, a slow, delicate kiss that made her insides turn to baby-pink marshmallow.

'What you did...telling me about our baby...was very brave, Adele. You knew it was risky, but you did it anyway, out of love for me, because I had asked you to be open. And I responded with extreme cowardice by running in the opposite direction.'

She pulled her mouth into a crinkly smile. 'But you came back...again. I just can't get rid of you, can I?'

'Nope.' His face, so serious a few moments before, broke into a wide grin.

Over the next hour or so they wandered round the property making plans, daring to dream things they'd both thought forever put on hold. Adele drove Nick home and during the journey they chatted excitedly about renovating the farm and planned for the future.

It was almost like old times. Almost.

Adele smiled to herself. This time it was better. There was a deeper connection than had ever been there before and a deeper understanding of each other. They might be complete opposites, but this time they were going to make their differences work for them, rather than against them.

Later that evening Adele wandered out into the garden of their London house in her bathrobe. She would be sad to leave this place, but the idea of renovating the farmhouse and having Nick working next door sounded fantastic. He'd even pointed out a little dairy that he'd thought could be turned into an office for her.

The frosty air clung to her skin, but the moon was full and large as it rose in the dusky lavender sky. She wanted to stand out here and look at it for a while. It seemed to be shining full of possibilities.

Nick came up behind her and circled his arms round her waist. She leant back into him, relishing the warmth he was giving out.

'Beautiful, isn't it?' she said.

'That's because it's magic hour.'

Uh-oh. She could feel one of Nick's cheesy one-liners coming on. She'd just have to head him off at the pass.

'I thought you said it was all to do with colour temperature and stuff like that. Seems like plain old physics to me. Nothing magical about that.'

Nick traced a line of kisses down the side of her neck and all the little hairs there started to tingle.

'How about this?' he murmured. 'Any magic there?'

She smiled and let her eyes drift closed.

'Promising.'

Nick backed away and tugged at her hand. A cold rush of air hit the space where he had been. He raised just one eyebrow.

'I think you'd better come inside and let me show you just how magical the next hour—or possibly more—could be.'

And then he was gone, leaving the patio door open as an invitation.

Rats! She'd walked right into that one.

Still, it didn't stop her running into the house after him. She wasn't sure she could perform magic, but Nick had been spot-on—when the two of them got it right, it was wonderful.

0507 Gen Std HB

JUNE 2007 HARDBACK TITLES

ROMANCE™

Taken: the Spaniard's Virgin *Lucy Monroe*	978 0 263 19636 8
The Petrakos Bride *Lynne Graham*	978 0 263 19637 5
The Brazilian Boss's Innocent Mistress *Sarah Morgan*	
	978 0 263 19638 2
For the Sheikh's Pleasure *Annie West*	978 0 263 19639 9
The Greek Prince's Chosen Wife *Sandra Marton*	
	978 0 263 19640 5
Bedded at His Convenience *Margaret Mayo*	978 0 263 19641 2
The Billionaire's Marriage Bargain *Carole Mortimer*	
	978 0 263 19642 9
The Greek Billionaire's Baby Revenge *Jennie Lucas*	
	978 0 263 19643 6
The Italian's Wife by Sunset *Lucy Gordon*	978 0 263 19644 3
Reunited: Marriage in a Million *Liz Fielding*	978 0 263 19645 0
His Miracle Bride *Marion Lennox*	978 0 263 19646 7
Break Up to Make Up *Fiona Harper*	978 0 263 19647 4
Marrying Her Billionaire Boss *Myrna Mackenzie*	
	978 0 263 19648 1
Baby Twins: Parents Needed *Teresa Carpenter*	978 0 263 19649 8
The Italian GP's Bride *Kate Hardy*	978 0 263 19650 4
The Doctor's Pregnancy Secret *Leah Martyn*	978 0 263 19651 1

HISTORICAL ROMANCE™

No Place For a Lady *Louise Allen*	978 0 263 19763 1
Bride of the Solway *Joanna Maitland*	978 0 263 19764 8
Marianne and the Marquis *Anne Herries*	978 0 263 19765 5

MEDICAL ROMANCE™

The Consultant's Italian Knight *Maggie Kingsley*	
	978 0 263 19804 1
Her Man of Honour *Melanie Milburne*	978 0 263 19805 8
One Special Night... *Margaret McDonagh*	978 0 263 19806 5
Bride for a Single Dad *Laura Iding*	978 0 263 19807 2

MILLS & BOON®

0507 Gen Std LP

JUNE 2007 LARGE PRINT TITLES

ROMANCE™

Taken by the Sheikh *Penny Jordan*	978 0 263 19455 5
The Greek's Virgin *Trish Morey*	978 0 263 19456 2
The Forced Bride *Sara Craven*	978 0 263 19457 9
Bedded and Wedded for Revenge *Melanie Milburne*	
	978 0 263 19458 6
Rancher and Protector *Judy Christenberry*	978 0 263 19459 3
The Valentine Bride *Liz Fielding*	978 0 263 19460 9
One Summer in Italy... *Lucy Gordon*	978 0 263 19461 6
Crowned: An Ordinary Girl *Natasha Oakley*	978 0 263 19462 3

HISTORICAL ROMANCE™

The Wanton Bride *Mary Brendan*	978 0 263 19394 7
A Scandalous Mistress *Juliet Landon*	978 0 263 19395 4
A Wealthy Widow *Anne Herries*	978 0 263 19396 1

MEDICAL ROMANCE™

The Midwife's Christmas Miracle *Sarah Morgan*	978 0 263 19351 0
One Night To Wed *Alison Roberts*	978 0 263 19352 7
A Very Special Proposal *Josie Metcalfe*	978 0 263 19353 4
The Surgeon's Meant-To-Be Bride *Amy Andrews*	
	978 0 263 19354 1
A Father By Christmas *Meredith Webber*	978 0 263 19551 4
A Mother for His Baby *Leah Martyn*	978 0 263 19552 1

MILLS & BOON®

JULY 2007 HARDBACK TITLES

ROMANCE™

Blackmailed into the Italian's Bed *Miranda Lee* 978 0 263 19652 8
The Greek Tycoon's Pregnant Wife *Anne Mather*
978 0 263 19653 5
Innocent on Her Wedding Night *Sara Craven* 978 0 263 19654 2
The Spanish Duke's Virgin Bride *Chantelle Shaw*
978 0 263 19655 9
The Mediterranean Billionaire's Secret Baby *Diana Hamilton*
978 0 263 19656 6
The Boss's Wife for a Week *Anne McAllister* 978 0 263 19657 3
The Kouros Marriage Revenge *Abby Green* 978 0 263 19658 0
Jed Hunter's Reluctant Bride *Susanne James* 978 0 263 19659 7
Promoted: Nanny to Wife *Margaret Way* 978 0 263 19660 3
Needed: Her Mr Right *Barbara Hannay* 978 0 263 19661 0
Outback Boss, City Bride *Jessica Hart* 978 0 263 19662 7
The Bridal Contract *Susan Fox* 978 0 263 19663 4
Marriage at Circle M *Donna Alward* 978 0 263 19664 1
The Italian Single Dad *Jennie Adams* 978 0 263 19665 8
The Single Dad's Marriage Wish *Carol Marinelli*
978 0 263 19666 5
The Surgeon's Runaway Bride *Olivia Gates* 978 0 263 19667 2

HISTORICAL ROMANCE™

A Desirable Husband *Mary Nichols* 978 0 263 19766 2
His Cinderella Bride *Annie Burrows* 978 0 263 19767 9
Tamed By the Barbarian *June Francis* 978 0 263 19768 6

MEDICAL ROMANCE™

The Playboy Doctor's Proposal *Alison Roberts* 978 0 263 19808 9
The Consultant's Surprise Child *Joanna Neil* 978 0 263 19809 6
Dr Ferrero's Baby Secret *Jennifer Taylor* 978 0 263 19810 2
Their Very Special Child *Dianne Drake* 978 0 263 19811 9

MILLS & BOON®

0607 Gen Std LP

JULY 2007 LARGE PRINT TITLES

ROMANCE™

Royally Bedded, Regally Wedded *Julia James*	978 0 263 19463 0
The Sheikh's English Bride *Sharon Kendrick*	978 0 263 19464 7
Sicilian Husband, Blackmailed Bride *Kate Walker*	
	978 0 263 19465 4
At the Greek Boss's Bidding *Jane Porter*	978 0 263 19466 1
Cattle Rancher, Convenient Wife *Margaret Way*	
	978 0 263 19467 8
Barefoot Bride *Jessica Hart*	978 0 263 19468 5
Their Very Special Gift *Jackie Braun*	978 0 263 19469 2
Her Parenthood Assignment *Fiona Harper*	978 0 263 19470 8

HISTORICAL ROMANCE™

Innocence and Impropriety *Diane Gaston*	978 0 263 19397 8
Rogue's Widow, Gentleman's Wife *Helen Dickson*	
	978 0 263 19398 5
High Seas To High Society *Sophia James*	978 0 263 19399 2

MEDICAL ROMANCE™

The Surgeon's Miracle Baby *Carol Marinelli*	978 0 263 19355 8
A Consultant Claims His Bride *Maggie Kingsley*	
	978 0 263 19356 5
The Woman He's Been Waiting For *Jennifer Taylor*	
	978 0 263 19357 2
The Village Doctor's Marriage *Abigail Gordon*	978 0 263 19358 9
In Her Boss's Special Care *Melanie Milburne*	978 0 263 19554 5
The Surgeon's Courageous Bride *Lucy Clark*	978 0 263 19555 2